MAKE US GODS THAT SHALL GO BEFORE US

- Exodus 32:1 NKJV

A Haunting Tale of Idolatry and Influence

MAKE US GODS THAT SHALL GO BEFORE US

A Haunting Tale of Idolatry and Influence

DAWN NICOLE EVANS

This book is a work of fiction. Although, all biblical scriptures referenced from the *Holy Bible* are true and noted from the *New King James Version,* all other characters, names, titles, programs, organizations and places are designed and depicted from the author's imagination or understanding of the *Holy Bible* and used in a fictitious manner. Any resemblance to actual persons, living or dead, or businesses or institutions active or inactive is purely coincidental.

Also note, this work is Christian fiction and any depictions of lifestyles, dialogue, or situations that are seemingly contrary to that of a Christian identity are necessary for the establishment of characters and story.

Dedications

I thank God for giving me the courage and wisdom to do this again and for guiding me through new territory and bringing me out wiser on the other side.

Thank you, Mom and Dad, for all the books and for never holding me back from God's plan.

Thank you, New Gal Publishing for the previous works we collaborated on and all that you taught me along the way.

"They served their idols, which became a snare to them. They even sacrificed their sons and their daughters to demons, and shed innocent blood, the blood of their sons and daughters, whom they sacrificed to the idols of Canaan; and the land was polluted with blood. Thus they were defiled by their own works, and played the harlot by their own deeds."

PSALM 106: 36-39 (NKJV)

PROLOGUE: WHAT THE ENEMY MEANT FOR EVIL …

"God is what you make Him out to be." Argo Stoddard whispered to himself. It was cold and dark in the office when he broke in; though technically, he had a key so he was not exactly *breaking* in. It would be accurate to say that he was in the office when he was not supposed to be. In fact, Argo was not supposed to be on the lot at all, even though he had founded the entire studio decades earlier.

"What blasphemous talk from my son," Argo spat. "God is not made, but the Maker and no thing that is made can be a god. I'll bet you don't agree though?" Argo asked the miniature gold statue in the center of the fully detailed display of the future theme park: Oliver's Island. The park was Argo's dream, which his son Arthur stole, after pulling a coup and taking over the studio. Arthur also took control of Argo's original productions, including his flagship series *Oliver's Explorations*; the most popular children's show in the country and the foundation of the entire theme park.

Arthur was the one moving forward with construction of the park after making a significant change to Argo's original design. At the same time, Arthur was trying to keep Argo unaware of the changes to *Oliver's Explorations* by banning his father from the studio lot and this office, which was formerly Argo's office.

"Of course you don't agree," Argo continued to taunt the statue, knowing that it could not or would not respond. "Because you think you're a god, but you're not. You are a creation, not a creator, but all the children worship you anyway." He whispered as he flicked the miniature with the tip of his finger. The gold miniature was just a model of the larger statue made for the theme park. The statue was a new design, or *reimagining* as Arthur called it, of Miranda the Mermaid; the puppet mermaid that was once Argo's muse and the mascot of *Oliver's Explorations* and Stoddard Pictures.

Then somehow, at some point, what Argo created began to overtake him and he was no longer the creator, but a slave to his own creation. Now, tonight, the night before his birthday celebration, Argo planned to take back his freedom and that of every child who was under Miranda's spell. Just like a siren she had become, Miranda the Mermaid, luring the children in with her songs of diversity and inclusion, only to drown them in dangerous waters of bodily harm, perversity and rebellion.

"I am not ashamed we're not the same," Miranda's small voice sang and Argo covered his ears but he could not shut the voice out as the singing was inside of him; stuck in his head for weeks and growing louder and louder at the most awkward and inconvenient times.

"I love our differences, they make us shine!" The voice grew deeper, as it was no longer the original Miranda's sweet and melodious soprano but something different, something dangerous.

"You can cut all that singing off right now because I'm not under any spell of yours!" Argo replied in his most commanding tone, but the singer seemed unfazed by his declaration. Still, Argo would not back down either, instead he spoke directly to the miniature statue on the display, "I see right through you, and my son would too if he wasn't so blinded by greed!" Argo cried out but no one was listening. "The love of money truly is a root of all kinds of evil, as the good book says."[1] Argo added mournfully. His son Arthur was not always so bad and perhaps it was because of Argo spoiling him that the boy turned out the way he did? Arthur did not intend for his son to become such a terrible man, but Argo's wife, Victoria died soon after giving birth to their son and it was important to Argo that his son knew what a treasure he was to him. All the gifts and the trips, the expensive toys and advanced schools did nothing more than turn Arthur into a self-centered, entitled brat who could never see the true value in anything, especially hard work. In fact, since grade school, Arthur was always trying to make a profit off the work of other people. It was as if Arthur's only talent was to leech off another's creative gifts and somehow profit.

In Argo's case, he did not take action against his son soon enough to protect the production company Argo started. Now Argo figured his son must have felt a little guilty because Arthur was planning this big birthday party for Argo tomorrow night, where Arthur also planned to reveal to the world the premiere episode of the new season of *Oliver's Explorations* and the new Miranda the Mermaid.

At seventy, Argo may have been a little confused at times but he was not stupid, the party was not just to ease what little conscience Arthur had, but it was also a weak attempt by Arthur to convince the world that Argo was *for* the changes Arthur made to the show and not adamantly *against* them. If Arthur could get his father Argo, nicknamed "Papa Argo" by fans across the nation, to approve of what Arthur was doing to the show, the parents of the fans would not question the content. Arthur refused to take part in parents blindly allowing their children to fall prey to abominations.

---

[1] 1 TIMOTHY 6:10 (NKJV)

Argo was not silent about his disproval to whoever would listen, but now he intended to do something about it himself. As much as he hated to see Oliver come to an end, it was better that the show end now, under Argo's terms, then to continue for even another season spreading that woke garbage like some kind of cancer.

"Dad you have to let this go," Arthur explained to his father just days prior, when they had a brief conversation at Stoddard Manor. "There is nothing wrong with the changes we're making to the show. We are drawing in more viewers this way and opening the doors for a wider market. What you started was good, and you should be proud of that, but it's outdated now and somewhat regressive. Now as far as Scotty is concerned, I'm sorry I didn't tell you earlier, but he didn't want to renew his contract and I think it's for the best, he's getting too old to play Oliver. I mean he's almost an adult." Arthur explained, though he would not look at his father directly when he spoke of Scotty and Argo knew his son was lying to him. That was the routine of their conversations, what few they still had in the years since Arthur put Argo in a private nursing home after taking over the studio.

"Of course he didn't want to renew his contract, look what you are doing to his character, turning Oliver into a …" Argo was still alone in the office, thinking about how he should have replied to his son, yet he still could not bring himself to say the words aloud. It really made no sense to Argo to replace Oliver of *Oliver's Explorations* as Scotty Colman would always be Oliver to the fans and it was his explorations. Argo could do nothing to stop young Scott from being let go ahead of the next season. While Arthur claimed the issue was with Scotty not wanting to renew his contract, Argo suspected otherwise, as he did not trust that man his son hired years ago to be the new show-runner after Arthur fired everyone who worked with Argo from the show's pilot episode. Allan Teague brought all this perversity in and while Argo had not seen him do anything out of the ordinary, he still did not want that man around the children. What kind of man gets little boys to do that sort of thing and calls it acting or entertainment? Argo was so desperate to stop all the madness he even tried to convince Scott's mother to help him get Teague off the show. That woman was just as bad as Arthur was, all she cared about was money, if she were younger, Arthur would've been chasing after her too as Argo's son refused to commit to anyone, including his own current wife.

"What's good for me is good for me, what's good for you is good for you." The voice returned in the strange baritone to remind Argo it had not let up in any way on driving him insane. Argo began to hate that song, and he was the one who wrote it!

"What's good for you?" Argo muttered while shaking his head. "You don't know what's good for you or anyone else. You're not even real; you're a puppet, the imaginary friend of a little orphan boy! I made you up! What do you know about what's good for anyone?" Argo shouted at the display with growing fury over the corruption of his creation. This was supposed to be his theme park, at least the one he dreamed up when he was a young man just starting out in puppetry. Argo wanted to make a place that catered toward children in a fun and wholesome way, just as the show was supposed to do. A place where children could be happy and play and their parents did not have to worry about the cost of tickets, food or souvenirs. In fact, Argo planned to give out free tickets to children in foster care and families with parents who were on government assistance programs and most likely could not afford such trips, as he saw no reason why any child should be excluded from the park. Argo also planned to give out toys every day to every child who visited the park. Argo loved all children as if they were his own, but he was cursed with one biological child, an ungrateful son that Argo made the mistake of spoiling rotten and lived long enough to regret it.

Arthur did not seem to know about anything except money and womanizing, often using the former to get the latter. Arthur's first wife Lydia was an actress that Arthur only married because he liked what he saw at the time. Argo tried to warn his son not to base his relationships by looks, but character and actual love. Of course, Arthur did not bother with his father's advice but settled for superficial attraction and within a few years, Arthur began to complain about how his starlet wife was letting herself go. The two had one daughter together, Argo's first grandchild and a sort of namesake, little Margo. Argo had hoped becoming a father himself would calm his son down but it only seemed to make him worse in character, as Arthur was almost never home and carried on many affairs with different women. Margo was barely 18 at the time of her parent's divorce and only a few years younger than her father's mistress was at the time, a young woman named Paige, whom he married just months later after she gave birth to his son A.J.

Argo loved both his grandchildren and subtly wished that he had more, albeit he would rather they came into the world under more conventional circumstances, but he wouldn't love them any less either way. The issue was that Arthur didn't enjoy being a father or a husband and Argo suspected his son had forced more than one young woman he was involved with to abort a pregnancy. It pained Argo greatly to even think about what a dreadful person his son was. Arthur seemed to have absolutely no compassion for anyone, neither for his own family or the children he exploited with the show. If only Argo's wife Victoria were still alive, things might have been different. Argo liked to believe that if she had not died, he would have taken a better stance against Arthur while the boy was growing up, instead of catering to his son's every want because of his guilt.

Argo examined the display of Oliver's Island theme park, which was to begin construction the following year and the entire set up was near exact to how Argo sketched it years ago except for one thing, that monstrosity of a statue in the center of it all. This was not what Argo dreamed up when he designed the park. He wanted the waterslides, the grotto, and the boat tours on Oliver's pirate ship Kalypso. He wanted the BBQ restaurant that served authentic island food and the novelty shops full of toys, costumes and figurines; but that statue, that statue was a mockery of everything *Oliver's Explorations* originally stood for. It was a mutation of not only the original Miranda, but of Argo's legacy.

"As long as we do what just makes us happy!" The strange voice belted out suddenly. Finishing off the opening theme song of *Oliver's Explorations* just as Argo snatched the little gold model statue from the center of the miniature display and threw it to the floor. He tried to stomp on it but his old worn out sneakers were not strong enough to break it and the figure was jabbing into the bottom of his foot so that it was doing more irritation to him than he was doing to it. Argo brought his foot down on the figurine once again anyway, though this time at a bad angle and he lost his balance. He fell to the floor and the figurine bounced across the carpet away from him and landed under the desk.

Argo was crawling on the floor to retrieve the miniature when his son Arthur entered the office from the hall elevators. Arthur's office was the only one on the top floor, and the only room from any level of the building with a perfect view of the production lot only a short block away.

"Dad, what are you doing in here? You should be asleep back at the manor! And how did you even get down here?" Arthur asked just as Argo retrieved the figure from the floor and quickly got back on his feet. Argo looked out the window briefly then looked at his son and noticed immediately the smell of perfume emanating from Arthur's casual attire. Arthur must have been in the building with one of his "lady-friends" the whole time. Perhaps in the lobby or one of the other offices, because when he addressed Argo he sounded angry but not panicked and seemed completely ignorant to what was happening on the lot just outside his window.

"Dad, I asked you a question, what are you doing in here?" Arthur growled, as he was not in any mood for his father's antics tonight. Before Argo could respond, Arthur noticed the display for Oliver's Island had been disturbed and the gold statue from the center was missing.

"What did you do to the model Dad?" Arthur demanded an answer from his father as Argo tried to slip past him and out the door with the miniature in his hand. Arthur grabbed his father by the shoulders aggressively to stop him before he fled the office. Arthur knew he never should have trusted a lone nurse to watch his father overnight in the manor.

After his father, Argo received a diagnosis of early stage dementia, Arthur had him moved to a private nursing home with a team of nurses and doctors treating him. However, for the night before his dad's birthday party and the premiere of the new season of *Oliver*, Arthur thought it was a good idea to bring his dad back to the manor house with only one nurse and minimal supplies, as Arthur did not want his own home looking like a hospital. The old man could not even make it through one night peacefully. It was important to Arthur that the celebration went on without issue, as he planned to introduce the *new* Miranda the Mermaid and announce Scott's replacement. Arthur had enough trouble trying to convince the fans that the show was still safe under Arthur's direction and the show-runner Allan Teague. Some people were still very critical and opposing of the changes to the series after the shift in power a few years back and Arthur was careful not to let his father near the studio or in front of a camera anymore and now he saw that was for good reason.

"Dad, what did you do to the display?" Arthur asked while he tried to open Argo's fist.

"I did what I needed to. You've made *Oliver's Explorations* into an abomination and I won't stand for it. The next generation doesn't need this!" Argo screamed at his son and Arthur grabbed his father's frail arms and forced the old man to sit down in the chair by the display.

"We talked about this; it's not an abomination, it is change! Everything is modernizing all around you and this studio needs to catch up! I don't even understand why you're complaining. I'm opening the theme park you always wanted!" Arthur explained his voice full of frustration as he motioned to the display directly in front of Argo.

"That is not my park and this is not my dream!" Argo hissed as he thrust the miniature in his son's face. "This is an abomination and a perversion of what I've worked for, not to mention a perversion of the human body!" Argo shouted back, although the body in question was that of a mermaid, sort of, Argo still felt he made his point accurately enough. Infuriated and exhausted, the elderly man tossed the gold miniature of the new Miranda at his son. Arthur caught the miniature statue in his hand and sighed. Arthur walked over to the display, returned the miniature to its place and frowned at his father.

"Listen to me you need to get over this. I'm trying to revive your dream here and make it relevant again. Allan Teague is trying to …" Argo interrupted his son by spitting on the floor in disgust at just the mention of the show-runner's name.

"Trying to make filth under my name is what he's doing! And I don't trust him around the children!" Argo added and Arthur's face grew red with anger.

"What is the matter with you? Listen to the way you're talking right now. If any of your fans heard you saying things like that you think they'd still admire you. Don't make assumptions about the man because of his private life. You don't know anything about him except that he's gay. I swear you act like judge and jury for everyone who isn't exactly like you. Thanks to Allan we've got our first multicultural cast lined up for the next season, under you that never would've happened!" Arthur argued.

"I'm not a racist! I don't hate people for their skin; I hate them for what they do!" Argo fired back, clearly offended by the suggestion. Arthur stood up straight, as sirens blared in the distance outside on the street below, to show his father would not intimidate him. In fact, he always treated his father dismissively, ever since he was a teenager and realized he could do whatever he wanted. Arthur looked down on Argo as if Argo were his child and not the other way around.

"I'm not going to debate this with you because I don't have to. This is my production company now, I brought Allan on, and he is not going anywhere. Scotty is too old to play Oliver anymore and it's time for him to move on and for the cast to expand in a better direction." Arthur explained slowly as if talking to his wife or some other imbecile.

"You mean he's too old for Teague's taste." Argo shot back in disgust, but Arthur dismissed the comment.

"The point is that *Oliver's Explorations* is going in a new direction, a better direction. I thought you'd be proud of me, I'm turning your dream into a reality and this studio into an empire." Arthur replied, slightly offended by his father's ungrateful attitude, at least he was still taking care of his old man which was more than Argo deserved in his opinion. Arthur did all this for Argo, well maybe not all of it was for Argo. He wanted his father to see that he could carry the torch for the Stoddard name and make it into something more. Arthur's landline on the desk rang and he turned away to answer it but stopped when Argo started talking again.

"My son, I realized too late that I failed you; in all that I've done that is what I am greatly sorry for. I never taught you that empires fall and some of them fall hard. You are making those children bow to an idol, a false god, a siren that promises great many things but in the end, she will only take. You made Miranda into something that is going to destroy the lives of so many children and you think you will profit off their lives, but it's going to cost you your own legacy, your very own children and grandchildren will suffer for this as a sacrifice and you'll regret your choices in hell. I will not sit quietly and have my name on such abominations." Argo explained softly and Arthur looked at his father in complete disbelief. The phone stopped ringing but started again though Arthur did not go to pick it up immediately as he had to take a moment to process how badly his father's mental health had declined. The doctor warned Arthur that Argo would see things and hear things that were not there. That he would say strange or cruel things and could even become violent. Arthur never imagined that any of those things would come true but here he was seeing it for himself.

"Dad, I hope that one day you can understand that what I'm doing now is for the greater good and the Stoddard name." Arthur explained. More sirens blared from the street below as Argo stood up and crossed the room to cup his son's face gently in his hands.

"My son that is exactly what I was going to say to you." Argo replied just as the phone rang again. "You should answer that." Argo added as he shuffled to the door. Arthur watched his father curiously, as he lifted the landline receiver and pressed it to his ear. Before Arthur could say a word, someone was screaming on the other end.

"Dad … Dad it's burning, it's all burning!" Arthur's daughter Margo screamed as Arthur could hear the same sirens from the street earlier, much clearer now, almost as if they were right next to him. Arthur looked out the window to see his soundstage was on fire. This was the same soundstage where they filmed *Oliver's Explorations*; the largest structure on the lot, now engulfed in flames. Arthur inhaled sharply and dropped the phone before he crossed the office, pressed his hands against the cool glass of the window and stared in shock at the large fire.

The soundstage was where the celebration was to take place tomorrow night. It was to begin with an exclusive viewing of the premiere episode to the new season that would be Scott's last and would conclude with the unveiling of the new Miranda. There were six children invited to the exclusive event, all selected as finalists in the auditions to become the new Oliver. The one casted would take Scott's place in the next season. Scott and Argo were not happy about the change and while Arthur did not care at the time; now the cogs were beginning to turn in his mind. His own father may have orchestrated all this damage to slow down production but it was unlikely the old man had set an entire building on fire on his own.

"What have you done old man? Do you have any idea how much this is going to cost me?" Arthur asked.

"I know the costs very well young man, do you?" Argo asked before he turned to leave but stopped as if he remembered something else. "You know many kings and emperors believed they were greater than God too or that they could make themselves into gods, and yet whatever power they thought they had did not stop their kingdoms and empires from becoming nothing more than rubble in human history. You might rebuild son, in fact, I know you'll try, but I take comfort in the knowledge that like other arrogant leaders such as yourself, your new empire will not profit you as this one once did." Argo added before leaving the office and a stunned Arthur.

CHAPTER ONE

"Scott, I really think you should join your family in the visiting room?" Dr. Greer's voice breaks the awkward silence of what would be their final session together. While there should have been relief on Scott's part, he knew his release was not on his own terms, but due to his inability to pay for further care out of pocket and Dr. Greer's inability to accept defeat. If Scott was not ready to go home, which he was not, Greer was going to do everything she could to make him believe that he *was* ready and healed. Greer would do anything to avoid tarnishing her reputation as Scott's continuing issues might cast doubt upon her unconventional methods of therapy and psychiatric treatment. Greer's career priorities and practices were neither appropriate nor productive to her profession according to Scott, but at the same time they were not uncommon, as Scott had seen the same lack of compassion and inflated ego in Greer that he'd seen in every other therapist he'd been treated by in over 20 years. The only reason he returned to Greer after all this time was that he did not know where else to go.

"Scott they came a long way to see you. This situation is just as painful for them as it is for you." Greer adds. Still, Scott refuses to look into the observation window knowing exactly what he is going to see and knowing it is all for show. The visiting room, or "family room" at the hospital, was a simple square box of a room with hideous salmon pink walls barely visible beneath the haphazardly taped children's drawings like poorly hung wallpaper. The furniture in the room consisted of a single child-size round table with three child-size chairs; a furnishing technique meant to add to the discomfort of the room as a whole, while supplying a nice odd number of seats to increase the chance of excluding someone from a visit. The room was supposed to be comforting and welcoming, like a real family room but it was the exact opposite, not just because of the terrible choice in décor but also due to the large and obvious two-way mirror on the wall, which allowed people on Scott's side to gawk at everyone on the other side. The family room was in fact more like an observation room or more accurately, a fish bowl.

Unlike most visitors, Scott's family does not seem to notice the two-way mirror at all, except his oldest daughter Kieri. While her side of the mirror is simply just a mirror and she cannot see her dad, Scott still feels like she knows he is there; which is why Scott did not want to look up and accidentally make eye contact. He begged his doctor not to invite his family up here but Greer did it anyway in her bid to force him to pretend everything was all right. He was not cured or improved and he had not resolved any of his issues in any way; in fact, he was not even having a major breakthrough with his mental health. He was back at square one or perhaps he was even worse off now than if he had been back at square one. To be fair, Scott didn't completely blame Greer for expelling him from the hospital now, as Scott himself would expect to get paid for his work if he were doing any and he knew going in that Greer and her clinic didn't take charity cases. What angered him more than anything was that Greer was sending him away and acting as if she had accomplished something, when she had not done anything at all in the time Scott was under her care.

"Scott you told me recently that you regretted your last conversation with your eldest daughter. You admitted that you felt bad about the things you said to her and you were angry and hurt about the things she said to you. I want you to consider how you'll feel if you miss this opportunity to at least talk to your daughter now; and how you felt not having that same opportunity with your childhood friend whom you never saw again." Greer explains and Scott chews his bottom lip.

"I remember what I said." Scott replies simply, as it almost hurts to talk.

"Then you also remember how the guilt weighed on you." Greer adds impatiently. She is probably late for a lunch date, or a meeting with her publisher, she only ever used guilt tactics like bringing up Scott's best friend Grayson when she was frustrated with him. When Scott was 19, his friend and co-star, Grayson Lind committed suicide and Scott always regretted not doing something to stop him. Scott believed that if he had been a more mature person at the time he could have let the past go and Grayson might still be alive.

"I don't know why you keep bringing that up as if something can be done about it now. Grayson is dead and talking to my daughter won't change that. I asked you not to invite my family up here because I am still not in a good place mentally to be a decent husband or father, and you're acting as if everything is just fine now because I get to see Kieri again. Do you have any idea how much I hate this place? By coming back here I was doing what I was told to do whenever I felt like I couldn't hold on anymore; and now you're kicking me out because I can't pay and your pride won't let you admit that you failed." Scott accuses.

"Scott, I'm sending you home because that's where you belong, with your family." Greer argues calmly, though she cannot hide her face, which has gone red either from embarrassment or from anger or both.

"I can't face her! This isn't just about what I said to her, it's about what I did. I sent her away; I tried to relocate my daughter, as a person would do to a pet they don't want anymore. That's not something you can just apologize for and it's not something that can be easily forgiven." Scott replies.

"You *can* apologize for such a thing; it's just extremely difficult and painful to do so and even more painful and difficult to forgive, but it's not impossible. Moreover, you won't know if Kieri forgives you or not unless you talk to her. I think the fact that she's even here now is enough to show you she's not angry or bitter toward you. She said things that hurt and so did you, but sadly, that is something that happens among family all the time. There is no perfect way of navigating parenthood and I think Kieri is mature enough to understand that. You're in what could be a more complicated position with your adopted children and there is no amount of classes to take or books to read or videos and tutorials to watch that can make adopting and raising a child any easier but you're doing what you can. No one has the right to judge you for it, they will, but they don't have the right to." Greer explains and Scott cannot argue with her anymore. Instead, he lifts his head slowly and looks into the window; Kieri is staring straight at him, exactly where she can sense he is. It startles him that Kieri can be so blindly accurate and he believes for a moment that maybe she *can* see him. She does not look angry or sad or even upset at all, her expression is more of a curious nature.

Scott's window into the visiting room has a familiar feel to it, reminding Scott of his days on the set of live-tapings to shows other than his own. One show in particular about a blended family, had scenes that took place primarily in a living room, complete with the obviously organized disarray of the decor to appear lived in and welcoming, but instead achieved a look that was less like a home and more like the staged scene it really was. Like any other set, Scott's eyes wander to the dark corners of the office window, searching for what's hidden in the shadows beyond the picture perfect scene that is meant to distract him. From his perspective now, Scott can see more clearly the inaccuracies in the once perfect vision of his family. This revelation left him questioning why one of his children was dead and the other had turned against him. This scene, this moment, made him question why, if there was a God, He would choose to save someone like Scott while killing someone like Grayson at the same time?

Scott rises abruptly out of the chair to leave the room, but two orderlies blocking the door interrupt his dramatic exit. Scott looks to Greer who stares back at him in confusion. Scott raises his hands in frustration.

"You told me to go in and see my family; I can't do that if you don't let me out of the room!" Scott explains sharply. Surprised and possibly believing her berating of him has worked somehow, Greer motions for the orderlies to escort Scott next door into the family room. Outside in the overly lit, not so sterile looking hallway, Scott has a moment to rethink what he is doing. This was sure to be another bad decision added to his list of regrets, one more among so many.

CHAPTER TWO

A pothole in the road rocks the car only slightly, but the sudden shift is strong enough to cause Kieri's head to bump against the window gently and wake her from her dream about Kaila. She dreamt about the day she and her twin had gone swimming at the public pool. For any other 12 year olds, that would've been a normal summer event, but things got awkward while the twins were in the bathroom changing and a woman called the police and Kaila started arguing with everyone until their parents arrived to take the twins back home. That was three years ago and to this day Kieri would not return to that city pool.

Now that she is awake, Kieri shivers when her body registers how cold it is inside the car. It's nearly pitch black outside her window aside from the head and tail lights of the car and Kieri checks the time on her phone, noting that it's nearly 10 p.m. and she has no cell service. This road did not look anything like the vibrant town they left when they got off the plane. Beside her, Kieri's younger sister Riah is asleep in her car seat with her favorite blue blanket having fallen off of her and landing in a pile on the floor beneath her feet. Kieri retrieves the blanket and covers her sister up again before searching the floor for her own coat. It was warm when they got off the plane in town and Kieri can recall tossing her coat in the trunk of the rental car with her suitcase. Kieri scowls and presses her face between the front seats to watch her parents riding silently, her Papa Scott is driving as usual and staring straight ahead.

She had not spoken much to her father since his return home from the psych ward nearly a week earlier. They did not really have the time to talk about what happened, as everything was moving so quickly. Kieri's grandfather, whom she never met, had died recently and now they had to go to his big house in the middle of nowhere for some kind of memorial and for Kieri and Riah to meet their aunt for the first time. Though the situation caused the family to have to make a sudden trip out of town, it was not as if Kieri and Scott did not have opportunities prior to leaving home to talk to one another, but how does someone discuss a thing like sending your child away? Admittedly, Kieri felt just as ashamed about the issue, considering what she'd done and said that led to her being sent away in the first place. Neither her nor Scott was bold enough to start a real conversation on the topic, so they spent a week drifting around one another with trivial conversations or minimal communication altogether and keeping themselves occupied with the minor details of the trip.

Kieri looks out the backseat window again and squints hard trying to make out anything on the dark road; it seems their car is the only one out tonight.

"Doesn't anyone else live out here?" Kieri asks, breaking the silence in the car and her Papa AJ lets out a little yelp while holding his hand to his chest dramatically.

"You nearly gave me a heart attack! I thought you were still asleep!" Her Papa AJ replies.

"I was asleep, until that speed bump or whatever it was shook the car and woke me up." Kieri explains.

"It was a pothole; sorry I was trying to avoid them but this road is pretty terrible." Papa Scott clarifies from the driver seat but Papa AJ does not acknowledge him. Papa AJ looks at Kieri and smiles.

"Sorry about that sweetie, what did you ask me just now?" Papa AJ asks.

"I asked if anyone else lives out here. There are no cars behind us or in front of us and I don't see any houses on this road." Kieri says.

"No one lives out here except my sister Margo now. The reason you don't see any other cars is that this is a private road. It belongs to the Stoddard Estate and only leads to Stoddard Manor. Only Stoddard family members, employees of the estate and invited guests are allowed this far in. You won't see any other houses aside from the manor because the rest of the land is nothing but trees. I'm not sure if there is a direct path or trail through it, but I think the trees lining this road might eventually connect back to the woods behind Stoddard Manor. If we have the time while we're here, you and I can hike it together." AJ suggests with a smile and Kieri looks excited.

"So all this land belonged to your dad, even the road? Why would he need that much property if it was just him and your sister?" Kieri asks.

"Well you know how rich people are; they just have to do everything big." AJ explains in jest at first. "Actually this property all belonged to my Grandfather Argo first; then when he got sick, my father took over production of *Oliver's Explorations*, the entire studio and this property. Grandpa bought up all this land and had a house built on it because he wanted a big family. He was very traditional like that. He was born in a time when you could raise fourteen kids on a single income." AJ explains.

"So you have aunts and uncles?" Kieri asks optimistically as she had never met any extended family from either of her fathers, but AJ shakes his head sadly.

"No, actually grandpa only had one child, my Dad, Arthur." AJ explains.

"And he kept all this property anyway, even though he didn't need all the room?" Kieri asks just as Scott makes a right turn into a roundabout driveway that is lit up with little lights on the ground and a large fountain in the center.

"Oh yeah, grandpa kept his hopes up for more children or at least a few more grandchildren but by the time he realized it would only ever be Margo and myself, my dad had taken over everything and built himself an empire. My dad loved the seclusion of this place." AJ explains as Scott parks directly in front of the house.

"I think the correct word you're looking for is *exclusion*." Scott quips. AJ frowns at his husband before he climbs out of the car. As Kieri is about to ask what her dad means about exclusion, she is caught off guard by the sight of the manor house. The place is huge, larger than the entire apartment complex her family was currently living in. Kieri thought their old condominium was a luxury but this place left her speechless.

The manor is only two stories high but makes up for the lack of height in massive width. Every window of every front facing room has a light on, illuminating the entire structure like a large beacon in the surrounding darkness. Kieri stares in awe at the mansion as the front double doors open up wide and an elderly woman dressed in a tight black cocktail dress, makes her way quickly down the stairs in a pair of black stilettos on very sharp tips, while squealing with delight.

"Oh, my baby brother has arrived!" Margo shouts. She reaches the driveway at the same time as AJ to greet him. The two embrace as Scott begins to unlock Riah from her car seat. Kieri remains beside the car watching her Papa AJ and newly discovered Aunt Margo hug and kiss in excitement. "You look so handsome, look at you all grown up and living your best life, and I love the facial hair it completes you somehow." Margo adds playfully as she rubs her manicured nails over AJ's beard, which he had taken to growing out while Scott was away.

"Margo you're still a character. I'm glad old age hasn't changed you a bit." AJ replies with a not-so-subtle mocking tone as he appraises Margo's outfit. Margo lets the comment roll off her back as AJ leads her with his arm around her thin waist toward the car where Kieri is standing. Margo looks at Kieri and smiles wide.

"Well hello beautiful. My goodness, I can't believe I actually have nieces." Margo gushes as she hugs Kieri tight. Scott approaches with Riah still asleep in his arms. "And I think I still remember this handsome gentleman." Margo says playfully as she hugs her brother-in-law.

"This is the baby, Riah." Scott says as he presents the sleeping toddler to Margo who kisses her gently on the forehead leaving a heavy red lipstick print on her dark brown skin.

"Kieri and Riah," Margo pronounces each name slowly, almost as if she is reading their names out phonetically. "I got it and I won't forget it." Margo promises as she turns back to the house.

"Where's the valet?" AJ asks as he looks around expecting someone to appear any minute.

"Just leave your car here for now and you can get your bags out later." Margo directs and AJ looks offended.

"Why do we have to do it ourselves? Can't the valet bring the bags in before they park the car in the garage?" AJ asks and Margo frowns.

"Baby brother you're such a snob, I swear you've never done a bit of manual labor in your life. Dad got rid of the valet years ago; in fact, he got rid of all the employees, it was a waste of money keeping them on. No one works here now, except *me*." Margo remarks sarcastically as she turns back toward the house but stops when she realizes her guests are not following her. "It will be fine AJ, we can have dinner first and after that I'm pretty sure at least one of you strong young men will be fully capable of parking the car in the garage without the help of a valet. If you're careful you won't ruin your manicure bringing your own bags in the house. Now all of you come inside as I have a very special guest I want you to meet." Margo exclaims as she wraps an arm around Kieri's shoulders and leads her into the house, followed by Scott who is carrying Riah and AJ who looks mournfully back at the car before following the rest inside.

CHAPTER THREE

"So how long have you and my sister been seeing each other, Tristan?" AJ asks the much younger man in an abrasive tone. AJ was not going to play dumb for Margo's sake, as he knew exactly why this con man, who was about 40 years his sister's junior, was hanging around. After their arrival, which became that much more awkward by Margo's overcompensating kindness due to her distance over the years, AJ's older sister brought them all inside for a very late dinner. Tristan was waiting in the dining room with all his false charm and immediately introduced himself as Margo's new boyfriend. Did Margo even realize how ridiculous she looked dating a man who was young enough to be her grandson? After another round of awkward greetings, Scott put Riah down in one of the guest bedrooms and the adults, along with Kieri, sat down to eat and catch up. Margo sat at one end of the table with Tristan to her left so they could giggle and flirt and make everyone else nauseous; on Tristan's left, at the other end of the table sat AJ. Scott was beside AJ, across from Tristan and Kieri was beside Scott on Margo's right side.

"We've been together almost three weeks now?" Tristan replies with a confident smile and a quick kiss on Margo's cheek as if he believes that to be some sort of relationship milestone and perhaps for Tristan, it is. "According to her that's not enough time for us to run off together and get married but I'm not going to stop proposing until I wear her down." Tristan adds. Margo blushes as she addresses the rest of the table.

"I don't have any business getting married again. I've learned that marriage is the worst thing a person could do in a relationship, it takes all the passion out of the equation and you're just left with … each other."

Margo jokes though she and Tristan seem to be the only ones who get the punch line.

"How is Bob by the way?" AJ asks. Margo frowns at the mention of her ex-husband.

"I wouldn't know, I didn't get my annual Christmas card full of updates on his life this year, but I did get my monthly alimony check so I know he's still employed, which is all that matters to me." Margo replies confidently. She raises her glass for a toast and even AJ cannot help but join in.

"You shouldn't have let that man sour you on traditional marriage." Tristan continues on the subject. "One day we could be like your brother and his hubby, married with kids of our own." Tristan adds. Scott chokes on his wine for a second and he sets his glass down to wipe his mouth with a napkin.

"Sorry, this wine is a little strong." Scott explains sheepishly, his face flush with embarrassment. AJ covers his own mouth with his wine glass so Margo cannot see him laughing but she gives her brother a sharp look anyway.

"I guess my little brother is the more traditional of the two of us. Settling down and starting a beautiful family. You're very lucky Junior." Margo replies solemnly and raises her glass for another toast, as before, the rest of the adults at the table follow suit as Kieri watches on in confusion.

"You know I hate when you call me that, but thank you for the compliment." AJ replies as he smiles at Margo from across the table.

"Speaking of relationships, how did you two meet?" Tristan asks Scott but before AJ can answer for him, Margo nudges Tristan.

"Darling, I told you this story already." Margo reminds him gently. Tristan smiles at her but does not back down from his question.

"You did tell me, but I want to hear it again, from the source." Tristan replies before motioning to Scott with his fork. "So, how did you two meet?" Tristan asks again. Scott shrugs and looks at AJ.

"AJ and I sort of grew up together. We fell out of touch for a while and reconnected as adults." Scott's simple reply leaves Tristan looking on expectantly.

"That's it? How boring, it sounds just like how *straight* people meet?" Tristan says and AJ quickly interjects.

"Is there something wrong with gay men meeting like two boring, *straight* people? Maybe we like boring." AJ replies sharply. Tristan stares at him, unfazed.

"Maybe he does," Tristan motions to Scott, "but you don't strike me as the type of guy who likes boring." Tristan replies to AJ casually.

"He doesn't mean anything by it. I think I just told your story a little more dramatically that's all." Margo interjects to ease the tension at the table.

"He can speak for himself." Scott counters.

"Come on, don't get like that, it's not a homophobic thing. I just figured you two would've had a more exciting story. I don't have a problem with gays; I almost played a gay character in a movie. If I had gotten the part, I would've brought so much passion to that role, you would've seen me on the red carpet during award season taking home my gold. I mean back then anyway, playing a simple gay character now isn't as award-worthy as it used to be." Tristan explains. Scott and AJ give each other a look but say nothing at first and AJ concedes to lighten up the conversation by clarifying a little more on his relationship with Scott.

"As Scott said and I'm sure Margo already told you, Scott and I first met when we were kids. I was visiting my grandfather's studio for the first time. Scott played Oliver on the kid's show *Oliver's Explorations*. I'm sure it was before your time but you might have seen the reruns." AJ explains before taking a sip of his wine and glaring at his sister for forcing them to dine with this man. Tristan smiles anyway, completely oblivious to the terrible impression he is making on the family.

"Actually, now that you mention it, I think I have seen a couple of reruns of that show." Tristan admits to AJ before addressing Scott. "I bet it was awkward talking to that puppet mermaid?" Tristan adds and Scott shakes his head.

"Actually I enjoyed talking to Miranda; she was just about the nicest one on the set." Scott replies and Tristan laughs loudly though Scott was not completely joking.

"That's a good one. Well that's cool that you started your career so young. You know I've never seen you in anything else though, I mean you didn't do any more acting after that show ended?" Tristan asks as he reaches for the wine bottle, which Margo quickly pulls closer to her plate.

"Actually Scott is a music producer now with some big name clients, so he's still very busy since *Oliver* and I think you've had enough to drink for tonight." Margo chides playfully and Tristan raises his hands in surrender.

"Yes ma'am, anything for you." Tristan drunkenly replies to Margo. He smiles awkwardly as he addresses the rest of the table. "You see why I keep telling her she would make a great mother. I apologize if I said anything offensive; you two seem like good guys." Tristan adds.

"They are good guys. Sweetheart, did I tell you that my brother is a huge activist for equality of the LGTBQ community, especially in the entertainment industry." Margo explains with pride to fill the awkward transition in the conversation as AJ smiles wearily.

"Actually our eldest daughter Kaila was more the warrior, not me." AJ replies mournfully. Scott and Kieri look at him in unison but say nothing.

"Is that so?" Tristan addresses Kieri, "So you're a warrior, huh?" Tristan asks, seemingly oblivious to his mistake and Margo interjects quickly.

"Darling that's Kieri. I told you that Kaila passed away." Margo reminds him with an uncomfortable look and Tristan sobers up slightly.

"Sorry, Margo did tell me you had three kids. I just assumed …" Tristan looks at Kieri apologetically as he trails off.

"It's an understandable mistake, Kieri and Kaila were twins, they would both be 15 now and it's amazing how time flies. It seemed like just yesterday I was changing their diapers and trying to remember which one was which." AJ replies while forcing himself to laugh at his own cliché joke.

"I'm really sorry that I missed her funeral baby brother and that I wasn't there for you after everything that happened. I never should've let Dad push us apart." Margo replies, hesitantly adding an awkward, yet sympathetic smile.

"It's okay, we just had a small gathering and a memorial service and I know you had a lot going on with Dad." AJ replies to comfort her before addressing Scott and Kieri. "Margo was taking care of our father before he died and I can't think of a harder job than that. It's bad enough he was just mean for no reason when he was in the right state of mind, but in the end he was diagnosed with dementia, just like our grandfather." AJ explains.

"He was seeing things and talking to people that weren't even there and it was terrifying at first. For a while, I thought the house was haunted. I went through five nurses and he ran each of them off, demanding that I take care of him myself as he *made* himself my responsibility. He didn't care that I was practically starting all over again, coming out of that horrible divorce and honestly I don't believe AJ and I owed him anything at all. I mean I know it sounds cruel to talk about our father that way but he burned his own bridges, which is why he had no one willing to care for him when he got sick. I think everyone here can agree that parents are sometimes overrated." Margo looks at Kieri who looks down at her half-finished dinner.

"I agree." Scott mumbles as he picks at his food. Margo smiles appreciatively at Scott for backing her opinion.

"Thank you Scott, you understand what I mean. It's rare to find people who had a healthy upbringing. Considering the normal family dynamic of the past doesn't work anymore, if it ever did in the first place. I applaud you two for breaking social standards and doing what's best for you and your children. No one has the right to tell you two that you can't marry or raise children. I see these beautiful girls and they look healthy and happy and have everything they could ever want." Margo explains with a smile.

"Thank you for that Margo. It's refreshing to hear something other than hate." AJ replies. Tristan looks confused.

"What do you mean by hate?" Tristan asks AJ.

"Margo didn't tell you about my channel? I have an online platform. It started out as just a little quirk for posting videos here and there. When Scott and I first adopted Kieri and Kaila, they were nine months old and I wanted to document everything they did. Fatherhood was completely new to me and I would post videos of them as babies, and reach out to people occasionally for a little help and I got a lot of positive feedback and encouragement at first. I think the girls were around a year old when the fans saw Scott more consistently and realized we were a gay couple and I was no longer a lone, clueless white man raising his two black children, so there was a shift in the response I got after that. It was subtle at first but definitely there. By then I was starting to get the hang of fatherhood anyway so I evolved the channel a little. I started giving my own tutorials and advice on subjects like our daughter's natural hair care process and eventually I started getting offers to promote black hair and skin care products in my videos. Then I launched my own line of beauty products that were in most major retail stores across the country. The trolls were still there, but my fan base was growing so I didn't worry about it too much at the time. Still, people can say some pretty awful things when you're just trying to do the best you can and after a while something will get under the skin." AJ explains.

"Personally I believe all that homophobia nonsense was an excuse." Margo interjects. "People aren't showing you hate solely because the girls don't have a mom. This has less to do with sexual orientation and almost everything to do with race." Margo concludes.

"Margo I'm starting to think your boyfriend isn't the only one at the table who is drunk." Scott snaps at Margo who tries to defend her suggestion.

"I'm just being honest in what I see. Look at the world we live in, gay lifestyle is accepted now, even the church has caught up with the rest of the population; it's practically encouraged everywhere now." As Margo rants, Scott looks at Kieri who is staring intently at her unfinished dinner. "What's not accepted though, is a white couple adopting black children and why? Because you're proving that you are better parents than their own biological parents would've been." Margo explains with growing intensity.

"You know what Margo I think we need to change the subject." Scott interjects again but AJ backs Margo's claim this time.

"No, no Scott she's got a point. I'm tired of people asking why we didn't adopt white children and how black children belong with black parents. I mean some people accused us of adopting our daughters for clout." AJ explains.

"Exactly, but nobody wants to say out loud that most white couples, not all, but most, have the means and the resources to raise healthy children of any color. I'm not saying this to sound racist, but no one is asking why so many black parents give their children up in the first place? I mean look at this beautiful girl, who wouldn't want to raise her!" Margo continues while motioning to Kieri, until Scott slams his drinking glass down on the table, shattering the stem.

"Enough! Change the subject! And has it ever occurred to either of you that not all children in the system are given up by their parents willingly but taken away unwillingly?" Scott counters before addressing AJ directly. "And by the way, I remember a season when neither of us was a very good parent and all our children weren't happy and healthy." Scott replies and AJ looks away. Margo raises her hands in submission.

"I apologize. I didn't mean to start anything, it just really bothered me the way people were attacking you both online." Margo explains.

"Then maybe you should stop going online?" Scott suggests as he begins to clean the broken glass off the table and turns toward Kieri to apologize for his outburst. Margo turns to Kieri to apologize as well.

"I'm sorry Kieri. I didn't mean to say anything negative about black culture. I love black culture, your hair, your clothing and … and with skin like yours, when you get to be my age you'll still look 20." Margo replies playfully before returning her attention to her food.

"I still appreciate you standing up for me Margo." AJ replies.

"I should've stood up for you a long time ago; especially with our father. Looking back on it now, I don't know why I allowed father to intimidate me the way he did. I mean being his daughter didn't benefit me all that much, nepotism wasn't boosting my acting career any." Margo replies. "I should've walked away from it all like you did AJ. I bet my career would've gone much further if I had made my own decisions from the beginning." Margo says bitterly.

"Well what choice did I have but to walk away after I was kicked out?" AJ asks before addressing Tristan. "Growing up, our dad refused to let me appear on Oliver or even the spinoffs; as terrible and short-lived as they were, it still would've been something. I mean I always knew I had talent for the camera but Dad always wanted to hinder that in me because he knew I was gay. Things only got worse when I came out to him and he kicked me out; and he refused to let Margo and I have any contact with each other. Margo was the lucky one though. She's a horror film icon and she's got a huge fan base out of it." AJ adds encouragingly and Margo frowns at first but transitions quickly to a smile when she addresses Kieri.

"Well what about you young lady? I bet you could get your own career going by dropping your Papa Scott's name a few times, plenty of people still remember him." Margo suggests to Kieri who looks embarrassed.

"That's not going to happen anytime soon." Scott replies sharply before Kieri can answer and AJ exhales in frustration. Margo looks at Scott in surprise.

"This is not the time or the place for this discussion again Scott." AJ replies.

"It's not a discussion at all, the answer was and still is no! Our daughters are not going to be child actors." Scott replies with finality and the whole table goes silent.

"Am I missing something here because I feel like I just kicked a hornet's nest *again*?" Margo asks uncomfortably, but neither man responds as they stare each other down defiantly. "I didn't mean anything problematic by the suggestion. I just meant that I love the videos that AJ posts of the girls and I assumed they'd get into acting like you did Scott." Margo adds.

"Well they won't, not if I have anything to say about it and they don't need to as far as I'm concerned." Scott replies.

"It's not about *need* Scott, no one said that they needed to do this. It's about *want*, they like being in front of the camera and they're good at it and this is the chance of a lifetime." AJ explains and Scott looks away in frustration.

"What's the chance of a lifetime? What are you two talking about?" Margo asks.

"I'm talking about *Oliver's Explorations*." AJ answers simply and after a moment Margo seems to catch on.

"Are you talking about the reboot rumors?" Margo asks.

"Oh they are definitely more than just rumors. It's not just people wanting a reboot either; some fans want to see a continuation of the original show. You should see the online threads and discussion posts about it; people want the show back badly to continue where it left off. Someone contacted me recently about working up a script and maybe even crowd-funding, if need be, to reprise the show. The ideas bouncing around are so exciting, some of the best are focused on little Oliver Rightwood as an adult with a family of his own. This would continue the story arc Allan Teague started in the last two seasons." AJ says; cutting his explanation short as he, Margo and Scott all knew why there was no official final season of the show.

"That sounds amazing, actually that's not a bad idea at all, especially if Kieri and Riah could be on it as well." Margo adds adamantly but there is a subtle hesitation in her voice.

"The writers I'm talking to suggested the very same thing for the reprisal to have something more inclusive. It would be a grown up Oliver, who was a childhood favorite and a positive role model, now undoing the demonization of homosexuality, along with showing the joy of culturally mixed families, all in a setting to reach children with understanding. It would essentially be our lives on screen." AJ explains to both Margo and Tristan.

"No, it would be a scripted show, just like *Oliver's Explorations* and there is nothing real or accurate about either one of them." Scott replies as he stands up from the table with his plate and leaves the dining room. The rest of the table remains silent before Margo attempts to break up the awkwardness.

"Well, on a lighter note, I've got cheesecake for dessert." Margo announces with a smile and the rest of the table resumes eating dinner in silence.

CHAPTER FOUR

"The Lord is my shepherd; I shall not want. He makes me to lie down in green pastures; He leads me beside the still waters. He restores my soul;" Kieri holds Riah in her lap as she reads Psalm 23 to the frightened toddler, from a children's Bible with pictures of a shepherd and sheep to accompany the scripture. During dinner, Riah was alone, asleep in the guest bedroom and when things got awkward after Papa Scott stormed off, Kieri asked to be excused to check on her little sister, whom she found crying and looking lost and distraught in an unfamiliar bedroom. When Riah saw Kieri she jumped into her older sister's arms, feeling more secure but not completely calm.

In an effort to comfort her sister tonight, Kieri chanced pulling out the children's Bible, which she had to hide in her luggage from her fathers, and began reading to her sister from the book of Psalms, Psalm 23 in particular was Kieri's favorite. Riah rests her head on Kieri's shoulder as she is slowly calming down and she sucks her thumb while staring intently at the illustrations in the book.

"He leads me in the paths of righteousness for His name's sake. Yea, though I walk through the valley of the shadow of death, I will fear no evil; for You are with me; Your rod and Your staff, they comfort me." Kieri continues reading and Riah pulls her thumb out of her mouth to point at the book's illustration of a large shadow looming over the sheep to represent the shadow of death. Riah looks fearfully at Kieri but says nothing. Last year Papa Scott had commented on the fact that Riah was not as verbal as other children her age were, but really stuck to only a few words like Up, Down, Dada or Kiwi, which was the closest she could get to saying Kieri. Now while that was something, the fact that Riah could not or would not say anymore was concerning to her fathers. If she wanted something she would point to it or wiggle out of someone's grasp to get it on her own. Kieri studies the illustration of the shadow, which even for a children's book, was a little intimidating.

"Don't worry Riah you want to know something I learned about shadows?" Riah listens to Kieri intently as the older sister raises her hand in front of the bedside lamp to cast a shadow on the blank wall beside the bed. Kieri directs Riah to look at the shadow of her hand and to see how it grows bigger and smaller depending on how she moves it toward or away from the lamp light. "The shadow of my hand can make my hand seem bigger than it really is. The shadow of death makes itself bigger than it really is, to seem scarier than it really is. I learned that from my friend Mrs. B." As Kieri explains the shadows, Riah smiles at her. Kieri is unsure of whether her little sister understands or not, but takes her smile as a good sign. Kieri kisses Riah on her forehead in the same spot Aunt Margo left her lip print, which has since, been wiped away.

"I know you probably don't understand it now, but basically you don't have to be afraid of the shadows and you don't have to be afraid to be alone because God is always with you." Kieri explains gently to Riah before looking down at the Bible in her own hands. "Now if only I could believe that myself." Kieri whispers and Riah, sensing that her older sister is sad, hugs her. The bedroom door opens suddenly and Kieri shoves the Bible under her blankets. Her Papa Scott enters and looks surprised to see Kieri in the room.

"I'm sorry Kieri I thought you were still downstairs having dinner. I would've knocked first if I had known you were up here." Scott explains awkwardly. Kieri's recent transformation from child to teenage girl caught her fathers off guard. They were still struggling to navigate with an appropriate structure of giving Kieri privacy and personal space without making her feel self-conscious of her maturing body. This began around the time the twins were about 10 or 11 and their fathers agreed not to enter their bedroom without knocking first. Although they had no issues with Kieri and Kaila sharing a bedroom at that age, which contradicted the whole purpose of giving their daughter privacy and girl-space. Riah climbs out of Kieri's lap and runs to her father and Scott scoops her up quickly.

"It's okay Dad, I just came up here because I lost my appetite and figured I would just check on Riah and go to bed." Kieri explains while making sure she hid the Bible securely under the blanket.

"I guess we had the same idea. Listen, I don't want Riah keeping you up all night, so she can sleep in the other room with your dad and me. I'm sorry about the conversation today at dinner. I haven't seen Margo since I was a teenager, so I won't even try to vouch for her character but she didn't seem like such an ignorant person back when I first met her. I hope you don't feel uncomfortable in this house or around her now." Scott adds.

"I think I'll be okay, don't you always say people are entitled to their own opinion?" Kieri reminds him and Scott shrugs, regretting how his words have come back to bite him. "I guessed maybe she's just awkward around people. Dad did mention it was just her and their father in this house for years, maybe she hadn't had anyone to talk to for a while?" Kieri adds.

"You're a lot more understanding than I am kiddo." Scott replies.

"How long are we staying here anyway?" Kieri asks and Scott tries to think. AJ had not told him anything specific, just that he wanted the whole family to go up to visit Margo for a while.

"You know I'm not sure. I mean AJ really wanted us to be here with him and we should support him. I know he and Margo talk and act like they don't miss their own father or anything but deep down I think they're both hurting." Scott explains but Kieri is confused.

"Papa AJ said his dad kicked him out years ago and wouldn't let him or Aunt Margo have any contact with each other; if their dad was that mean, why would they miss him?" Kieri asks.

"Well that's what makes things a little complicated." Scott replies as he enters the room and shuts the door behind him for privacy. "That story your Papa AJ told your aunt's boyfriend was true of how we met, it was just paraphrased a little. Your dad and I did meet as kids on the set of the show and we became really good friends at first, but some time later there was an accident at the studio one night before a really big celebration and things changed, not so much between us but *for* us." Scott explains.

"You mean the fire? Papa AJ told me once about a soundstage burning down?" Kieri adds and Scott nods.

"That's the one. Some people, security and a few crew members got hurt enough to get paid off and the show went on hiatus at first as AJ's dad tried to rebuild the soundstage and get things back in order; but the show never came back for another season after that. They even hired a new actor to replace me but everything fell apart anyway and some people, namely your grandfather, believed the fire cursed the show somehow and he blamed me for the whole thing. He claimed I was bitter because they were replacing me and that I had set fire to the building and tried to destroy some valuables. I was angry about getting fired, but I didn't take it that far and he had no proof that I did it so I wasn't officially charged with anything but his accusations, and the rumors he started were enough to pretty much end my career in television. AJ and I fell out of touch after that, then a few years later we met up again as adults and we started seeing each other and his father was not happy about that." Scott explains bitterly.

"So Papa AJ's dad did disown him because he's gay?" Kieri asks. Scott shrugs and shakes his head.

"That's what AJ will claim and I know some people talk big about supporting the LGBTQ community until one of their own children comes out of the closet, but in Arthur's case, your grandfather I mean, in his case I think it was really just hatred towards me. I mean honestly after the fire, it did seem like the show was cursed, the whole production company as a matter of fact. They couldn't come up with any good content after that. Not a single new show that lasted beyond a season and what few movies they were producing were bombing. They even ripped off a few shows from other countries that did better elsewhere but failed under Stoddard Pictures. They were sued a few times for producing scripts that were optioned to them but they never paid the writers for them. Then there was the theme park based off *Oliver's Explorations* that Arthur was planning to build, but that never came to fruition either since the investors suddenly dropped out after the fire. As long as he made money, AJ's dad wouldn't have had a big issue with his son marrying another man; his issue was that *I* was that man." Scott explains.

"Is that why you won't do the reboot Dad keeps talking about?" Kieri asks and Scott shrugs.

"That's even more complicated and too long of a story for tonight." Scott replies. He carries Riah in one arm and prepares to close Kieri's door with his other arm but stops as if he wants to say something else. "Well…goodnight." Is all Scott can manage before shutting the door abruptly and feeling like a fool. There were some moments when he could talk to Kieri like old times and other moments when the past came back up to the surface and it hurt to even look at his daughter.

~

"I'm really sorry about dinner baby brother. You and Scott just got here and I've already got you arguing with each other." Margo says to AJ. She exhales the cigarette smoke and watches the trail float away into the dark night. After dinner, Tristan drove himself home, or more likely out to another late night party, in Margo's car and AJ and Margo decided to take a smoke break out in the garden that led into the woods behind the house.

"We were arguing long before we got up here. He seems to think that he has the final say on what our children do and he doesn't and I don't appreciate him acting like I'm not their father too." AJ replies in anger as he exhales the cigarette smoke. He tried to quit when Kieri and Kaila came along but whenever he was stressed out, he would quickly fall off the path.

"I'm guessing he's acting the same way about you all moving up here for good as well?" Margo asks and AJ shrugs.

"I wouldn't know because I didn't tell him." AJ replies. Margo looks at her brother in disappointment.

"AJ!" Margo begins to chastise him but AJ snaps back at her.

"Well what was I supposed to do? I can't talk to him about anything anymore. You just saw how he was at dinner when I brought up the revival and the new show is for his benefit just as much as the girls, but he doesn't care. So how am I supposed to tell him that we're losing our home, *again*?" AJ asks.

"Well you have to tell him something soon because I can't keep paying your rent on that place and considering the available empty rooms here, it really makes no sense." Margo explains as she stares out into the deep dark of the woods beyond the garden.

"I know Margo and I'm sorry. I don't understand how things got this bad. It's just that ever since Kaila's death," AJ pauses and rubs his hands over his face. "I think everything has gone wrong since we lost her. You know I'm still getting hate mail after nearly two years and no sponsor will touch my brand now. The distributors are gone, my sponsors are gone and my fans have vanished just like that." AJ snaps his fingers in the air for emphasis as he fights back tears.

"That's the cost of living your life in front of the camera sweetheart, as soon as something is out of place no one cares about the real story. Your fans will abandon you or some people will get closer to you just to drain whatever you have left. What about Scott and his music, I thought he was just taking a break after Kaila died?" Margo asks and AJ smirks as he draws from his cigarette again.

"He did say he was going to take a break and somehow that break turned into a retirement. I was still hoping he would bounce back at some point but that was before he had himself committed and we're lucky his artists didn't sue us for everything, not that they would've gotten much. Giving up our home was just the start of it; and poor Kieri, she just didn't know what to do anymore either. She couldn't even sleep in that room she used to share with her sister so we figured it was better to remove ourselves from a toxic environment and all the memories and downsize until things picked up. The only problem is that things still haven't picked up. Now this opportunity has come along and it could change everything but Scott wants nothing to do with it. I mean I'm not holding any delusions that this show would be a hit like the original but at least it's something and it might just get Kieri started on her own career path but Scott is just so selfish." AJ explains.

"I'm sure he has some other reasons for saying no besides being selfish." Margo replies in Scott's defense.

"Well of course he does, I mean it's kind of obvious that he's jealous too. When Scott was a kid, everyone knew his face and grew up wanting to be him, the orphan Oliver with his pirate ship and his best friend Miranda the Mermaid. Losing all that fame and admiration so suddenly can make a person very bitter, and after all those accusations Dad made about him, Scott says he was blacklisted from the industry. When we got together, he used to talk about how the show took his childhood from him and when he wasn't bankable or cute anymore, the industry just abandoned him. He couldn't get a role to save his life and it made him so angry, so different from when we were kids. Which I can understand considering the fact that there wasn't even any proof that he started that fire; but this time around it's not about him and someone new wants to put our daughters in front of the camera and I really think he's jealous of that. I mean I don't believe the reboot is really going to be about him or focus on Oliver all that much. They need him for the nostalgia, but really, it's about bringing something new to children's television that this generation can look to for encouragement. I mean how many children of color used to watch that show wanting a character they could relate to and feel included. Now someone wants to reboot the show using the same concept Dad began in the last season they filmed, adding a multicultural cast and Miranda becoming full on non-binary and changing their name to

Axel." AJ adds with excitement and Margo looks at him sharply but says nothing. "Can you imagine how many trans-children in the world want to see someone on screen that self-identifies just like them? Now the opportunity is presenting itself but Scott is just so stubborn." AJ explains as he sits on the small bench beside the rundown fence enclosing the garden. He stubs his cigarette out on the metal underside of the seat and Margo begins to circle the old fence scraping off the peeling white paint with her thumbnail.

"Did you ever tell Scott who started that fire?" Margo asks cautiously while staring out into the dark entrance of the woods beyond the garden again. AJ frowns.

"No, how would I tell him if I didn't even know?" AJ asks and Margo gives her brother another sharp look.

"AJ you know perfectly well who started that fire." Margo snaps.

"I know that our grandfather was going through a mental decline and couldn't be blamed for the things he did as I'm sure even he didn't know what he was doing. And they rebuilt the building remember, so what does it matter?" AJ replies, his eyes on the mud beneath his feet as he talks.

"Don't put on a front for me baby brother, you know that fire took out more than a building and the rebuilding of the sound stage did nothing to bring back the magic touch for storytelling that our family used to have." Margo replies.

"Which is why I want to do this reboot; I know how much Stoddard Pictures meant to Dad, it was more important to him than it was to Grandpa. Maybe back then I didn't fully believe in curses but I'm starting to see it now, which is why I'm trying to do something about it. Why not give Miranda some new life and introduce Axel to the world properly?"

AJ asks. Margo does not answer the question but instead changes direction.

"Well, you seem to have forgotten that I used to act too, in lesser known features that no decent person would ever bother to remake, though if they did, a part of me wouldn't mind it, especially if they wanted to include me. There is another part of me though that can see Scott's point of view on all this and even I have to admit being a victim of ageism at any age, hurts very much. I mean Scott was still a teenager by the time his career fell apart. I was just entering my 40s when I started getting casting calls for the crazy old woman roles in horror films while men twice my age were still playing action heroes and characters with depth in real films. It's a lot that actors give for entertainment when they care about their craft and at the end of the day it's not much that the industry gives back in return." Margo explains. "So I can understand why Scott would be hesitant about allowing your daughters into that sort of world. I'm sure he's just trying to be a good parent and I doubt this has anything to do with jealousy." Margo adds. AJ exhales deeply.

"Margo you're supposed to be on my side about all this." AJ replies.

"I am on your side; I'm always on your side. I'm just saying maybe he has his reasons for not wanting to come back; reasons that have nothing to do with jealousy. I mean to be honest it was a cheesy show to begin with. None of it was very imaginative and our father didn't care about that show or the studio, he only wanted to promote the show so he could use Miranda as some sort of brand mascot like every other anthropomorphic character idea, to sell merchandise. Our grandfather actually loved what he created and then Dad comes along and he's cashing in on the idea to build a children's entertainment empire and it just happened to lose its appeal pretty quickly; luckily before they got that stupid amusement park off the ground, what a disaster that would've been." Margo adds.

"If you were on my side you would understand how important all this is. I'm aware of how silly the show was, mainly because Grandpa was pretty basic at his execution of it, but in Dad's defense, he was trying to modernize it for a new era." AJ argues and Margo laughs.

"Modernize it? You mean with the introduction of the non-binary merperson Axel or are you talking about the islander boy Cody and his addition to the show? Personally, I think that Cody storyline was what really buried the show, not the fire. The audience may not have said it out loud but most parents wouldn't be okay with teaching their children that sort of thing." Margo replies.

"You know it's almost ironic that our father could come up with a storyline like that and then disown his own son years later for being gay." AJ replies bitterly and Margo rests a hand on his shoulder.

"That's not irony, that's hypocrisy." Margo corrects him. "And you know Allan Teague was the mastermind behind that ridiculous story arc along with the trans-mermaid stuff. Dad didn't care one way or the other what he was teaching little children, as long as it made him lots and lots of money. But having his own son fall under the same influence was another matter altogether, besides I think Dad's bigger issue was your choice of partners; of course you knew how much Dad hated Scott, which is why you dated him in the first place." Margo explains smugly and AJ frowns.

"That is not why I dated Scott. I love him and you make it sound like my sexual orientation was from a *bad* influence. I think having a show like Oliver with characters I could relate to helped me a lot back then, and

Allan Teague was a trailblazer for that story arc as far as I'm concerned." AJ replies.

"If you say so; so you really think this reboot is a good idea? I mean at the end of the day those fans of yours can put whatever script they want together but if it's dealing with Oliver, or Miranda or anything else that the Stoddard name still holds the rights too, they'll need my permission to do it." Margo explains and AJ prepares to argue but she cuts him off. "Permission that I'm willing to give if the right people are on board; all nostalgia aside, a reboot, or reprisal or whatever you're calling it, won't work without the original Oliver. As far as inclusion is concerned, if Kieri wants to do it then that's great, if not you'll need to get someone else. But according to your friend's script, was the islander boy, Cody still the other half of this barrier breaking duo?" Margo asks with a knowing smirk.

"He is, but we can work around that." AJ explains quickly. The original actor, Grayson Lind who played Cody was long dead.

"How do you plan to work around that? I mean I know Cody was only a side character on the show in the beginning, but he still developed a fan base of his own, some people still do his signature islander call." Margo replies playfully.

"Well, I know replacing an actor is a little tricky but I see no reason why I couldn't do it." AJ suggests and Margo laughs.

"And there it is; the real root of all this persistence." Margo replies and AJ blushes with embarrassment.

"Don't start Margo, my addition to the show would be done out of necessity. And I'm only suggesting myself for the role because it might be kind of fun for a family to be acting together, we could be to modern day television, what the Nelson's were to the fifties." AJ explains and Margo concedes.

"Whatever you say baby brother and I am here for you but if Scott isn't on board, neither am I. And considering how he acted at dinner, I doubt very much that this whole reboot is going any further." Margo replies. She tosses her cigarette in the muddy flowerbed and marches back into the house. AJ stares at the cigarette still glowing before he crushes it into the mud under his boot.

"We'll see about that." AJ says to himself.

CHAPTER FIVE

"I am not ashamed we're not the same," A soft voice sings. Scott pauses in the middle of the woods, listening intently for the next verse. "I love our differences they make us shine!" He knows this song! Scott is barefoot on the cobblestone path in the woods that leads back to the garden behind the manor. It must be midday, as rays of light pour down on him through the trees from directly overhead. Scott makes his way down the little path and deeper into the woods, drawing closer and closer to the voice.

"What's good for me is good for me," The voice continues and Scott sings along in a whisper as he steps out of the woods and onto a brightly lit beach. His toes sink into the hot sand as a cool breeze ruffles his pajamas; no, not his pajamas, instead, he is wearing his old boarding school uniform again. Not *his* school uniform, but *Oliver's* school uniform. Dark blue shorts and a white dress shirt with blue and red striped suspenders that match his tie and the lining of his blue blazer.

"What's good for you is good for you." The voice seems to carry in the breeze as Scott opens his jacket and stares down at his attire. He had not worn this outfit since the first season of the show when he was a child and yet the clothing fit his adult body. Schoolmaster Pierce would not be happy to see that Scott had lost his shoes again though. Who was Schoolmaster Pierce? He ran the school Oliver attended but Scott had only ever known the man by name and could not put a face to him. So why was Scott suddenly feeling anxious about this man knowing that he lost his shoes? Schoolmaster Pierce was a character on Oliver, though not really a character as no actor had ever played him on the show, aside from an occasional voice over echoing through the halls of the boarding school in the first season, otherwise he was merely a name that had no face, an antagonist to Oliver's protagonist development. He was described as a militant, and later revealed, religious man, who ruled his school with pure intimidation and fear. He forced each little orphan boy into complacency and absolute obedience to his laws with punishment and abuse as revealed in the later seasons of the show. As far as the schoolchildren were to understand it, Schoolmaster Pierce was god. With each new episode and description of the man, he seemed less and less human and nowhere near qualified to be within twenty yards of children.

In the pilot episode of the show, Oliver escapes the school after a severe beating from the schoolmaster for a "crime" that is not divulged until much later in the series when Cody is introduced. Oliver flees in such a panic he loses his shoes somewhere and ends up on an island that is unusually familiar to him. It is there that Oliver meets Miranda for the first time, the mermaid portrayed by a puppet on the show, who tells Oliver all about his parents who perished during a plague that hit the island and killed nearly every adult. There was an invasion on the island only months later and baby Oliver, along with a few other orphaned children were kidnapped and placed in a reformatory school to refine them and mold them from the savage islanders they once were, into upstanding citizens of the new world. Oliver would not be broken so easily and after learning about his inheritance of a large ship, The Kalypso, Oliver began to sail the world searching for some new adventure as he dreamed of one day freeing the other children from the never seen, Schoolmaster Pierce's evil clutches.

Scott searches the bright beach for the singer, whom he assumes is Miranda the Mermaid, but there on the coastline, a group of children sit with their backs to Scott as another figure is perched on a rock, playing a toy guitar and singing the song. This does not look quite like Miranda, but from the distance, Scott can tell it is another mermaid, a puppet mermaid in fact. This puppet is about the same size as Miranda but moving on its own as Scott cannot see any puppeteers behind the rock. The puppet mermaid sits back swinging her bright green tail, which Scott can see as he draws closer, has little flecks of sequins sewn on her puppet body to make her tail glitter like emeralds. The mermaid can see Scott and waits patiently for him to approach the rock as she strums the guitar, or at least mimes the guitar playing movements, as she has no individual fingers. The actual music is probably coming from speakers, which Scott cannot see, similar to how the original show did it. Scott pauses a few feet away from the group of children, little boys and girls all dressed in uniforms similar to Scott's own. The new puppet continues the tune to finish the ending of the song and Scott joins with the children just in time.

"As long as we do what just makes us happy!" The group finishes the song together. Scott sits down in the sand beside the children and studies the mermaid. Scott is a little disappointed that this was not his old friend Miranda. The mermaid singing resembles Miranda slightly though but with obvious differences.

"I didn't mean to interrupt, I was looking for my friend Miranda, she used to meet me here and we would sing that same song together." Scott explains. The unfamiliar mermaid smiles at him, then faces the children with a frown, her expression more vivid and life-like than Miranda, almost as if she had actual muscle movements.

"Young ones, did you hear that? Scotty said a bad word; does anyone know what the word was and why it was bad?" The new mermaid asks and all the children raise their hands. The new mermaid picks a young dark-haired girl in the front row sitting beside Scott.

"I know, I know. Scotty said the word *she* without first asking for your chosen pronouns." The little girl answers proudly and the puppet claps her … its material hands together in praise.

"That's right Suzie." The puppet confirms to the little girl and the rest of the children before addressing Scott. "Hello Scotty, I used to be Miranda, I just look different now because of my new chosen identity. I no longer walk according to the gender assigned to me at birth but now identify as non-binary. And I don't go by my dead name anymore; I go by Axel now and I'm not a mermaid anymore as that is gender specific but a merperson and my pronouns are they/them." The merperson replies defiantly but with an eerie smile that tries to come off as kind. Scott feels embarrassed and the children stare at him waiting for his response.

"Sorry, I didn't mean to misgender you. I was just looking for my old friend." Scott explains nervously and the merperson smiles.

"It's okay, you were ignorant on the issue, but I'm still your friend." Axel the Merperson addresses the children. "You see children when people are kind and humble after misgendering you, there is no need for aggression or anger, and friendship can blossom. As long as those friends remember one important thing …" Axel leans forward to signal all the children to finish the quote.

"Respect our pronouns!" The children shout in delight and Axel smiles. Axel swings their tail slowly while staring at Scott as Scott studies Axel in return who looks vaguely the same as Miranda, except now instead of her normal seaweed top, *they* are wearing a sort of mesh shroud that looks to be made out of an old fishing net wrapped heavily around their chest like binding. Their tail is still a bright, sparkling green but their long blonde hair is so sun-bleached it is nearly white and cut much shorter in an undercut style with a fade on one side. What did not change at all though was this beach, which is actually just one part of the rest of the island. After going on some adventure on The Kalypso, Oliver would always return to this island to visit Miranda and get advice from her about life and suggestions on where he should take his ship next.

"It's good to see you again … Axel. I'm sorry I was gone for so long and stopped coming by to visit." Scott adds awkwardly as he had only ever been in a situation like this once before in life and it was not something he wanted to repeat.

"It's okay Scotty, we always knew that someday you'd have to grow up and meet other people and life out at sea made that a little difficult, so don't feel bad about leaving. Although, I sometimes wish that *someday* wouldn't have come so soon." Axel explains. Scott suddenly feels an overwhelming sense of guilt for abandoning his best friend. He looks out into the sea where the ship he inherited is anchored not that far from the shoreline. He usually had to leave the ship there because the waters were too shallow this close to shore. He would anchor the ship and take a small boat in the rest of the way so that he and Miranda could sit together, but this time he had come in from the woods behind the manor. Stoddard Manor! Scott suddenly remembers that there is so much to catch up on with Miranda … or Axel.

"Axel, did you know that I'm married now, and I have a family? I have two beautiful daughters?" Scott explains with excitement and the other children stare at him. He wants to tell them so badly about his new life now. To tell them about how he is not an orphan anymore! He is not alone anymore!

"Scotty, I already know all that about you, and I'm very proud of you and they are very beautiful children. I also know that you had *three* beautiful daughters once. We're all very sorry about what happened to Kaila, aren't we children?" Axel asks the children who nod with expressions of sadness. "I wish that I could've met her and maybe helped her the way I helped you, the way I'm helping these children now." Axel explains with a comforting, though forced smile. Scott can feel the oncoming tears burning his eyes that he fights hard to hold back but Axel can tell. "I'm sorry to bring up such a sad subject Scotty, but I think it's why we're all here. A person can handle only so much death and loss before they completely break emotionally if they don't have a friend to turn to for help." Axel explains gently. Scott nods in agreement but says nothing.

"Just look at all the children here. They come to me for help when the world and mean people in charge reject them, just as they rejected you. Children here have the right to be themselves, like Samantha." Axel motions to a little girl on the opposite side of Scott, who looks vaguely like Riah only a few years older. "Samantha, are you a girl or a boy?" Axel asks Samantha, who begins to giggle along with the other children.

"I don't know." Samantha replies. Her smile revealing two missing front teeth as she and her nearby friends fall over in the sand still giggling.

"You mean you don't know *yet*. After you spend a little more time here, you'll get the chance to choose if you're a girl or a boy or something else entirely. The real world wouldn't give you that choice; it's a choice they wouldn't give to our friend Kaila either. What do we say to the world for doing that, kids?" Axel asks and the children begin to boo and give thumbs down. Scott raises his hand slowly and Axel motions for him to speak. Scott stares at Samantha and the innocent expression on her face gives him that feeling again that he had when Kaila first started transitioning, but just as he did back then he says nothing now directly about it and waits for the feeling to go away.

"Do you think it was my fault, what happened to Kaila?" Scott asks. He had never said this question aloud and the weight of it causes him to look away into the ocean, which is calmer now, and the motion of the water seems strangely timed, almost programmed.

"Children, Scotty wants to know if it was his fault that Kaila died. What do you all think?" Axel asks the children and they look to Axel for confirmation as the puppet shakes their head.

"No!" The children shout in unison.

"Of course it wasn't your fault Scotty. You were a great father to Kaila and still are a great father to Kieri and Riah. The world is full of hate and opinions and people with very narrow perspectives, saying two men can't raise children, and it's about race with them too you know? They hate you because they don't know you or what you are capable of and they assume that with the way you live you can't give love to children who need it." Axel replies as the nearby children pat Scott gently on the back to comfort him.

"It's not really the people that got to me. I just feel that I failed Kaila; actually, I know I did. I know it was my fault, so I don't even know why I'm asking. They were my pills that she took and then when AJ left us I just didn't know what to do, and I sent Kieri away! How could I do that to my own daughters? I failed them both!" Scott breaks down in anger at himself. The children listen to him intently, some of them with expressions of confusion.

"Scotty, you are a great father and AJ was wrong for leaving, but he did come back to you. He came back and brought you all back together again because he loves you and he knows what a good person you are." Axel explains and Scott scoffs.

"He came back for the sympathy of his remaining fans. And to call out the people he blamed for Kaila's death." Scott counters and Axel's face turns hard and hostile.

"It was their fault Scotty. People aren't accepting as they should be. Like our favorite song, we should never be ashamed that we're not like everyone else, our differences make us stand out and be beautiful in our own way." Axel replies as their tail sparkles even more in the sunlight.

"What about me sending Kieri away? What if Kieri was right?" Scott asks hesitantly.

"Kieri was not right!" Axel snaps and Scott looks up, alarmed slightly at their change in tone. "Kieri is a child who had no right to say the things she said. What does she know about raising children? What do any of those criticizing trolls know?" Axel asks. Axel speaks to the children. "Scotty's daughter Kieri follows a God that tries to force people to do things His way and that's really mean." Axel explains in a patronizing tone and the children begin to pout. One little boy raises his hand and Axel gestures for him to speak.

"Axel, why can't we all just do what we like to do?" The little boy asks and Axel smiles.

"That's a good question Kyle. The answer is that some people think they know everything and will try to tell us that they know what is good for us better than we do. Like the time you hugged that little boy on the playground and your teacher tried to tell your mother that you liked boys and that she should nurture that behavior and your mommy got mad at the teacher. Your teacher knew what was good for you but your mommy didn't, that's why you're here." Axel explains. Kyle frowns at first as if still trying to understand but he soon gives up and smiles when all the other children begin to pat him on the back.

"How can you say that? He's only what, four or five years old, how can his teacher just assume he likes boys because he hugged one? Maybe he just wanted to give his friend a hug?" Scott suggests and Axel gives him a stern look.

"Scotty, we already addressed how rude it is to assume someone else's identifying gender and it is just as rude to assume their sexual orientation or to question that orientation because it doesn't follow social norms. It is not very nice of you to suggest, instead of asking, if Kyle identifies as a boy or as heterosexual and we won't be addressing those things again. And age doesn't matter when it comes to self-discovery, isn't that right children?" Axel asks the children who all shout back excitedly. A tremor runs through Scott as he recalls Allan Teague speaking those same words to him during rehearsal for the show.

"I'm sorry; I'm just trying to understand what you're telling these kids. I mean it was one little hug, that's not that big of a deal to be deciding a child's sexual orientation from, and what about Samantha, what's wrong with her just being a girl like she was born? Kids sometimes want to explore things but that doesn't mean they want to change their whole identity. Kaila liked Kieri's shoes when he was … when she was little because they had flowers and glitter on them, that doesn't mean … I'm just saying, how can we know what's good for ourselves or even for our children, without having some kind of standard for good in the first place? How can a person know what's good beforehand and know what direction to go in? Maybe Kyle's mother was just doing what she thought was good for him, or her, or them?" Scott replies, clearly flustered, causing the children to stare at him.

"Scotty, please stop confusing the children." Axel replies while trying to hold back their anger but Scott will not let up.

"I'm the one who is confused and I think I'm asking valid questions. We can't just spend the rest of our lives following what's in style. Just because something is popular or suddenly accepted or even legal doesn't make it good or even healthy, physically or mentally." Scott argues and Axel scowls at him.

"Scotty, what's good for you is what makes you happy and you don't need some so-called Divine Creator like Kieri does to tell you what makes you happy or what is good." Axel explains.

"So if an abuser is happy abusing and a killer is happy killing, does that make what they do into something good?" Scott asks and Axel frowns.

"That's not fair, and you know perfectly well that's not what I'm talking about." Axel replies.

"AJ and I thought certain things were good for Kaila but they didn't make her happy, not really." Scott adds while staring at his boat, which seems to be getting smaller as if it is floating away but he is sure it is at the same distance it was when he arrived.

"Kaila *was* happy." Axel claims but Scott interrupts.

"Was she?" Scott asks bitterly.

"She was and wherever she is now, I believe she is still happy because she's free. She was too good for the real world; it's a harsh and cold place that refuses to let the non-conforming thrive." Axel explains and all the children nod slowly in agreement. "Scotty, I know you love Kieri, but she's very confused right now and at an age where she is easily manipulated. You should not take what Kieri says seriously. She needs your help the way Kaila did; you have to do something to help her see the truth, that there is nothing wrong with her family and whoever says differently is not someone she should follow. In the meantime, I'll be here for you whenever you need me. Don't worry Scotty everything is going to be alright now." Axel assures Scott with a smile before addressing the children. "Alright young ones, Axel has to go now but I'll be back tomorrow and we'll sing and play and have fun!" Axel promises excitedly before setting the guitar down and diving into the rising tide that looks too shallow but is somehow deep enough for the merperson to disappear in, their sparkling green tail whipping up once more above the surface before disappearing under the too blue waves.

When Scott opens his eyes its dark out and he sits up on the edge of the bed, setting his bare feet on the cold, wooden floor of the guest room. AJ is still asleep on the other side of the bed, while Riah's toddler body is between them with her limbs spread out like a starfish. Scott stands up slowly so as not to wake either of them and waits for his eyes to adjust to the large guest room. It is massive like a grand hotel and similar in furniture and décor as Margo wanted to go all out for their visit. Grabbing his phone off the dresser, Scott uses the light to slip out of the room and into the hallway. Kieri's bedroom is to Scott's left and he uses the light to navigate his way there to check on her.

Kaila's death was the most difficult thing they had ever experienced as a family and it did not help matters that they all chose separate ways to mourn. Scott fell into a depression and was operating mostly on autopilot, while AJ fled to one of his boyfriends, which Scott expected and he could handle, eventually. Kieri's response was the most unexpected even though AJ and Scott did not raise their daughters as atheist but in fact encouraged belief in something. Scott's mother was catholic but she never forced him to go to church as she hardly went herself and Scott assumed she just liked the religious image. Not pushing any real principles on him was about the only thing Scott felt his mother got right when it came to parenting. So it was the only thing Scott chose to imitate from her and AJ agreed it was best to treat their daughters the same way by letting them find their own spirituality if they chose that route at all. He never in a million years thought Kieri would pick Christianity or at least some version of it that was so severe and conservative. Perhaps Axel was right and Kieri did not understand the oppressive nature of what she was following?

Scott enters Kieri's room silently to find her fast asleep, even with the bedside lamp illuminated and shining brightly upon her face. Scott looks around the room, which Margo also went through great effort to decorate for Kieri's arrival but the teenage themes were a little outdated. Scott sits down in the middle of the floor and stares at his sleeping daughter, remembering when she was seven years old and had a severe case of bronchitis and he spent nearly a week sleeping on the floor of her bedroom, fearing that at any point in the night she would suddenly wake up unable to breathe. No one ever warned him of the hardships of parenting and he never really had a consistent, positive parental influence in his life to show him what to do. Scott's own father ran from responsibility when his mother was pregnant with him. From the moment Scott and AJ brought their children home, Scott feared that something, some random incident or accident might occur that would take his children from him. He never imagined that incident would be due to his own mistakes. From the moment he held Kieri in his arms, Scott knew he would die for his children; which was why the sudden change in her hurt him so much. They were so close once, Scott just could not understand why his daughter would suddenly believe in a doctrine that would separate such a happy, beautiful family and upend everything for them.

Scott can see the open book half hidden under Kieri's blankets and he reaches over to pull the children's Bible out slowly. Scott stares at the cover and sighs heavily. After Kaila's death and AJ's disappearance, Kieri began reading Bible stories to Riah at night before bed. At first, Scott did not have a problem with Kieri sharing the stories with her little sister if it helped them cope. Until Kieri started questioning her fathers' relationship and the floodgates opened, causing his once loving daughter to turn into a bigot. Scott stood up, closed the book in one hand, shut the bedroom lamp off with the other and slipped out of the room silently with the Bible tucked under his arm. It was not the first Bible of Kieri's that he had to throw out but he certainly hoped it was the last.

CHAPTER SIX

The next morning AJ decides to show Kieri the rest of the house or as much as they can see before they get tired of walking around the large property. Margo, Scott and Riah went into town to pick up his father's ashes and the whole idea of his father reduced to what could fit in a shoebox left AJ unsettled, so he chose to stay behind with Kieri and take his mind off things with a little tour. The manor had gone through a remodel in the years since his father had kicked him out and on AJ's last visit before his father died, he did not get to see much of what was changed. As he and Kieri make their way down the hall of the first floor, AJ names the various family members whose portraits adorn the walls.

"That's my grandfather Argo Stoddard, the one who created *Oliver's Explorations*. Margo used to say we looked a lot alike. What do you think?" Kieri examines the portrait of her great-grandfather and shakes her head while frowning; they both laugh and continue down the hallway. They stop at another portrait, this one slightly newer than the one of Argo Stoddard. "And this is your grandfather Arthur Stoddard, the last patriarch of Stoddard Manor." AJ explains with a little saltiness in his tone.

"Was he really such a bad man? I mean, was he cruel to you all the time, even before you told him you were gay?" Kieri asks and AJ smiles bitterly.

"He was always cold and distant, which was cruel enough. I don't think he really loved anyone, not his wives, his children, or even his own parents. I don't think there was any help for a man like him because he didn't want to know love. My grandfather was a much better father figure to me. Had he lived long enough to meet you he would've loved you and spoiled you and that's saying something for a man who was born during segregation. Some people tried to say my grandfather was racist because he didn't have a diverse cast on the original *Oliver*, but the memories I have of him were good and I never saw him being mean to anyone, he was especially kind to children, of any race. My father on the other hand, did have a diverse cast but he didn't do that out of love or in the spirit of equality. Come on, I want to show you something." AJ opens the door beside his father's portrait and leads Kieri into a large office.

"This was my father's office, and I was never allowed in here when I was young. The first time I ever snuck into this room was when he went on a business trip and I stole the key before he left. I was a teenager at the time and really bored." AJ reminisces as he sits down in the large, worn out black leather chair at the desk. Kieri examines the bookcase while AJ spins around in the chair playfully. There is another portrait of his father on the wall over his head. Kieri runs her fingers over the dust jackets of the books, recognizing a few titles from her summer reading list; she stops over a leather-bound book with a four-letter acronym embossed in gold at the base of the spine.

"It was a few months after my grandfather had died that I snuck in here again and found all this paperwork that belonged to my father and it was all about how my grandfather could no longer take care of himself because he supposedly had dementia. My father used whatever information he could find to have his own father deemed unfit to care for himself or to remain in control of the company he created. My dad conned his way into becoming head of operations for the entire studio and put his own father under 24-hour nursing care, keeping him drugged up and locked in his room until he eventually died." AJ explains and Kieri looks horrified.

"That's terrible! How could he do something like that?" Kieri asks, completely appalled by her grandfather's behavior. AJ merely shrugs.

"I told you what kind of man he was; my father didn't love anyone or anything, except money. His own father gave him the best of everything and he repaid the old man by turning him into a vegetable. However, karma got my father in the end as he went through his own mental decline and psychotic episodes before he died and he deserved every minute of it. If my grandfather continued running the studio back then, I don't believe *Oliver's Explorations* would've ended so abruptly and with so many unresolved story arcs. Even though my grandfather didn't completely agree with the direction the show was going in at first; I think he was more upset about what his son was taking from him. The show was his baby, he made it for children around the world to enjoy and in the end, my grandfather would've come around and continued with the changes anyway, all he needed was the chance to see the positive aspect of the stories. Now we have to rely on recycling old content from back then to make new content today." AJ explains.

"I thought you wanted Dad to do the reboot? Isn't that like recycling old content too?" Kieri asks, as she pulls the leather-bound book from the shelf slowly. The inside flap has the name *Lydia Stoddard* written across it in beautiful cursive.

"Well yes and no. I mean this idea is more like a revival instead of a reboot of *Oliver's Explorations*. If we kept everything the same and started it all again from the beginning it would be poor recycling and laziness, but this is just continuing a story that should not have ended the way it did in the first place. Picking up where we left off to create another season that should've happened." AJ explains.

"If the show was so popular, what did happen? I mean didn't it seem strange to you that the show would come to an end because of a fire?" Kieri asks.

"Oh, absolutely, I mean a fire is only supposed to destroy tangible things. The only thing of value in the building at the time of the fire was my father's birthday gift to my grandfather; a statue Dad had made in commemoration of the show and the upcoming theme park. My father was going to present it to his dad at the premiere of the new season, then put the statue up in the center of the theme park when it was completed. After the fire the statue was damaged and a few people got hurt and the studio got sued and everything else seemed to go downhill from there and no one could figure out why." AJ explains. "Of course your Aunt Margo seems to think the ruin of Stoddard Pictures had more to do with the new showrunner at the time introducing the islander boy Cody as the love interest for Oliver." AJ explains and Kieri grimaces as she turns away from AJ though he notices anyway.

"So I guess you think the gay angle is why the show ended too?" AJ asks Kieri. She shrugs as she places the leather-bound book back on the shelf.

"I don't know; it just seems a little extra to put something like that on a children's show. It's kind of a mature storyline." Kieri explains carefully while remembering the last time she said too much to one of her fathers.

"Well, bullying starts in school, so school age seems to be the best time to teach tolerance." AJ replies, while recalling Scott's explanation of why he sent Kieri away.

"How is making two little boys kiss each other teaching tolerance? How is it even entertainment?" Kieri asks and AJ looks at her with surprise.

"*Making* them kiss? You do remember who played Oliver right. Your father knew who he was back then, and they weren't kids, they were about your age and didn't you remind me just recently that you're only three years away from being an adult and old enough to make your own decisions. You know who you are now and so did your father back then." AJ explains playfully to cover up his irritation at Kieri's comments. Kieri concedes with a shrug.

"Well I guess if Dad knew that he liked other men, or boys back then. It still seems like kind of a mature plot because it was a show for children and that might've been a little confusing for them." Kieri adds cautiously.

"Confusing or liberating?" AJ counters. Kieri does not reply but continues to look through the books. "You know if you like any of those books feel free to take one or two or fifty. I can promise you that Margo has never read any of them and won't anytime soon; and you know I'm more of a visual type who will pick a film or television show over the written word so someone might as well get some use out of that library while we're here." AJ suggests and Kieri smiles.

"Really? Thanks Dad." Kieri replies excitedly.

"Of course, anything for my girl; you don't know how grateful I am just to be able to watch you grow up. I miss our old videos and reading the comments from fans talking about how smart, beautiful, and talented you are. If only Kaila were still here so I could see the two of you together again. You know I used to be afraid that you felt like your Papa Scott and I treated you two differently." AJ adds.

"What do you mean?" Kieri asks. AJ shrugs and rises from the leather chair so he can sit on the edge of the desk.

"Well, being back here and being around Margo again just got me thinking about my father and though it was subtle, he treated Margo and me very differently. You see she and I have different mothers, sorry, different birthing persons and it was a constant reminder of the distance between us." AJ looks at Kieri and smiles apologetically. "I'm rambling aren't I? I guess what I mean to say is that Scott and I never wanted you or Kaila or Riah to feel like we loved any of you less than the others." AJ says. Kieri focuses intently on the books in front of her to fight back her emotions.

"I don't think that you love me any less." Kieri manages, but she has to stop herself from saying anymore.

"I'm glad to hear you say that. I was afraid for a long time that you felt shunned because you were jealous of Kaila and all the attention she was getting, especially during her transitioning." Kieri looks at AJ in surprise over the suggestion that she was ever jealous, but says nothing. He does not notice her expression as he is playing with a paperweight on the edge of the desk as he speaks. "I didn't mean to take the spotlight off of you in my videos, it was just important to show Kaila's journey to help other people." AJ explains. When AJ looks up from the desk, Kieri quickly looks away.

As a child, Kieri thought it was fun when her father would film her and her siblings. Then she reached a certain age when she realized that her Papa AJ was desperate for praise of any kind. AJ took to social media to prove to the world that two gay, white men were perfectly capable of raising three mentally, socially, physically and spiritually healthy black children. His videos gained a big following until Kaila's suicide, which led to accusations against AJ, that he was exploiting his children for clout. Some former subscribers claimed Kaila died because of a lack of a maternal figure and morals in the household. AJ fled from the backlash leaving Scott and Kieri to handle everything else. Riah was not even a year old at the time but even she could sense that something was wrong.

"I wasn't jealous of Kaila." Kieri replies softly.

"Sweetheart there is no shame in it. Siblings get envious of each other, it happens all the time. I admit I was jealous of Margo for years because of all the movies she did. Then I watched one and I realized there was no reason for me to be jealous. Of course I'll never say that to her face because it makes her feel good to think that I envy her." AJ explains.

"I wasn't jealous Dad." Kieri's response is more intense this time but AJ shrugs.

"Okay, I just wanted to be sure that you know how much your dad and I love you; and how badly we wanted you back. Although, there are some things that I really need you to understand if we're going to work as a family and heal together. When I was young, I really admired my dad, until I realized the kind of man he was. Like most Christians, he hid his own immoral ways behind religion, by judging other people and never examining himself." AJ explains. "He cut me off from the world I knew when I was barely an adult who didn't know anything about the ways of the world beyond these walls all because I wouldn't conform to what he wanted of me. I was so sheltered until then and had no idea what to do. My own mother didn't even try to stop him. Her husband was always more important than her son. My life with Paige taught me that mothers are overrated." It was rare for Kieri to hear her Papa AJ mention his mother and like always, it felt so strange and hostile. Kieri sits down on the edge of the desk beside her dad as AJ wipes his eyes with a tissue.

"I'm sorry your dad treated you like that." Kieri says and AJ wraps an arm over her shoulder.

"After my father disowned me I promised myself I would never be like him. I said that when I started a family my children would always know love, they would never be cast aside for any reason and I wouldn't hinder them from searching for what they want in life or treat them any different from each other and it was as if history just repeated itself anyway. When Scott sent you away, it wasn't that he didn't love you and it wasn't that he kept Riah because he loved her more. When I came back and you were gone, Scott was heartbroken but he didn't know what to do about it, which is why he had himself hospitalized again. I just hope that you can forgive us, both of us, because I'm just as much at fault as he is." Kieri looks down at her hands but says nothing. "And I understand that maybe it will take some time and a little giving from both sides. Scott told me about what you said to him and I don't want you to think that I'm defending his actions or saying that was a valid reason for him to send you away, because there is no valid reason for what he did; but I'd like you to consider putting yourself in his shoes. If someone you love told you that you were living wrong and that all the good you tried to do for them was worth nothing …" AJ begins and in frustration, Kieri interrupts him.

"That's not what I said! And that's not what I meant!" Kieri cries as she rises from the desk and AJ grabs her gently by the arms.

"Kieri, listen to me, what you said hurt him and it hurt me too. We sacrifice a lot for you girls and all we ask in return is that we strengthen each other as a family. If Kaila had your support back when she was transitioning, I think things would have been a lot easier for her and I'm not saying that any of this was your fault, because it wasn't. I just want you to understand how your words affect people." AJ says and Kieri inhales deeply over her father's not-so-subtle accusation. Did he really believe that Kieri's support for Kaila would have changed anything? He already believed Kieri was jealous of her twin and that that was why she did not support Kaila. "I'm glad that you found something to believe in, but the way you chose to cope is just not right. The things those people filled your head with to turn you against your own family was all wrong." AJ explains gently.

"The things you said to Scott were cruel," AJ continues. "Just like my father, just like the people who criticize your father and me for how we raise you. They don't know our lives, they don't know what we go through every day but they think they have the right to judge. That man!" AJ points at his father's portrait. "That man thought he had the right to judge me. He thought he had the right to condemn me for who I love as if he was following God himself. My father cheated on both his wives often and justified it. He was a crook who stole and manipulated for everything he ever had. He was a terrible human being who didn't care for human life. That is a Christian! That is what you're following! That man and people like him have no love for you. People like him call it a better world when one less person like you exists in it and that is whom you're taking the decisions of right and wrong. I am sure that there is a higher power out there somewhere Kieri, maybe even many, but the one I'm going to believe in is the one that brought us back together not the one that's trying to tear us apart. I just hope you can see the difference." AJ says. AJ exits the office leaving Kieri at the desk staring at the portrait, speechless.

CHAPTER SEVEN

Kieri knew what her Papa AJ said was not entirely true but his words brought on unwanted thoughts in her, causing her to question her beliefs. Faith was an everyday struggle for Kieri because she loved her dads very much but she could not let go of what she knew to be right and wrong and it hurt her how desperately her fathers wanted her to compromise somehow. Being raised in a family that was so far from God was difficult enough; but the fact that she was surrounded by and kept learning about people who claimed to be Christians but didn't act like it just complicated things for her.

When she was in elementary grade, Kieri and her twin attended a private school with the wealthy and privileged. The twins were prime targets for the other students, who mocked them for getting into the school on a POC scholarship. After Kaila's death, Kieri was enrolled in a public school for the first time and while the diversity was much more abundant there, the peace was not, as even the Christian kids there mocked Kieri all the time for having two fathers. The one positive aspect about her new public school was that Kieri was able to join the Bible study group and that was when she first heard the truth about God.

Outside of the group, it was hard for Kieri to learn anything more except for what she heard from some Christians on social media who did not do much talking about God but spent more time mocking and insulting families like Kieri's for their sinful lifestyles. One young man and his friends did video reviews every week about Papa AJ, Kaila, and the sick, twisted Stoddard clan. He and his friends would replay a video of Kaila and her transitioning and then make fun of what was going on, while vocalizing their belief that Kieri and her whole family were going to hell. Kieri realized that she was not learning anything about God from those videos and all they did was infuriate her. Though it did teach her that many so-called Christians didn't seem to know the definition of *following Christ* as Jesus didn't spend all his time mocking people. At least not in any Scriptures Kieri had ever read in the Bible.

While Kieri believed in God, sometimes she felt that He hated her and that there would be nothing more to her life besides pain and loss; and it did not help that the Bible she'd gotten from Mrs. B. at the group home had gone missing last night. She knew better than to leave it out like that but she fell asleep reading about Shadrach, Meshach and Abed-Nego in the book of Daniel. That story always scared her a little, mainly because she knew she was not as brave as they were. Was she willing to die for her faith when she was not even willing to stand up to her family? When she woke that morning, the Bible was gone and she was too afraid to ask her fathers about it. She knew they would get angry that she had it at all.

No matter how much Kieri tried, she could not convince her fathers that she was actually very grateful for them. She loved her family but she loved God too and that made things complicated for her. She knew how her family lived was wrong but she was too scared and too frustrated to do anything about it. Back at the youth home, Kieri had asked Mrs. B. an interesting question and the older woman's answer made a huge impact on Kieri in how she viewed things.

"Mrs. B, why did Jesus even bother?" Kieri asked as she and Mrs. B. were in the large dining hall setting up for a church function for local war veterans. Mrs. B. looked up from the table she was decorating.

"What do you mean? Why did He bother with what?" Mrs. B. asked.

"Why did He bother with any of us? Why did He come to earth and let Himself be beaten and brutalized and spit on just so people now could pretend He never existed in the first place?" Kieri asked in frustration. She'd been having a rough morning after her Papa AJ called her on the phone reassuring her that she'd be back home with him soon and while she missed Riah, Kieri wasn't all that positive she even wanted to go back.

"You've read the Bible. You know He did it because He loves us and if He didn't die for us we couldn't go to heaven to be with Him." Mrs. B. explained calmly, as always she was very patient with Kieri, answering her questions straight forward but not treating her like she was dumb.

"I know all that, I just mean, why did He bother to do it for everyone? He knew some people wouldn't believe and even the Bible says some people are still going to hell even though it's God's will for everyone to be saved. So why didn't Jesus just come for the ones He knew would receive salvation? Why did He suffer for the rest too?" Kieri asked as she set the placemats haphazardly on the tables for the luncheon.

Mrs. B. looked at Kieri for a moment, sat down on the bench at one of the tables and patted the seat beside her. Kieri collapsed in the seat and played with a placemat still in her hands.

"You're worried about going back aren't you?" Mrs. B. asked. Kieri could feel the anger welling up inside of her. She started to like it there with Mr. and Mrs. B. as the group home the couple ran felt like a safe place, it felt like a home. It was so different to see how affectionate Mr. and Mrs. B. were to each other compared to Kieri's fathers, who sometimes went whole days without saying a word to each other.

"Why can't I stay here? They don't really want me back and I'm not sure I even want to go." Kieri replied and Mrs. B. wrapped a comforting arm around her shoulders.

"You know Tommy and I have fostered children whose parents were in a bad place or struggling financially and they loved their kids. I could usually tell just in the way the children would talk about their lives and how much they missed their parents; and as far as I know, most of those kids never made it back to their loving parents and to this day, they might still be in the system. Then again, I have also fostered kids who lived under monsters, people simply devoid of sympathy, patience and kindness. Heartless individuals who did some of the worse things to their children that I could think of. Too often, those children had to return to those horrible homes because their parents knew how to play the system. So getting to know you and hearing the way you talk about your home life, I don't believe that your parents don't want you back. I believe they are in a bad spot and honestly think they are doing the right thing, so I hope that you don't believe that they hate you." Mrs. B. explained gently.

"As far as your question goes," Mrs. B. continues, "you asked why Jesus bothered with those that He knew wouldn't come to salvation. That makes me think of Abraham, in the book of Genesis, I think it was chapter 18 or 19 maybe, right before the destruction of Sodom and Gomorrah. God did not have to tell Abraham that He was going to destroy those cities, even in the text God is speaking about sharing this information with Abraham for a reason. The downfall of those terrible places was the result of the actions of the people who were completely distant from God, disregarding Him for worldly things, idols and immorality. Years ago I read that chapter and it hit me that perhaps God told Abraham what He was going to do so that Abraham would plead for the people of Sodom and Gomorrah, just as he did; which was strange to me because God knew what they were doing and whether or not they would stop. Yet still, He gave Abraham the opportunity as a single person to plead for those people, in a sense to pray intercession for those people so that they would not go to hell but repent and go to heaven." Mrs. B. rose from the bench, Kieri followed as Mrs. B. continued talking while they finished the tables.

"It was the compassion of Abraham to plead for people he didn't even know. That same compassion should be in all of us to pray for the people we do know. Of course, we know destruction rained down on Sodom and Gomorrah anyway and the only survivors were Lot and his two daughters. I think it's also important to remember that God promised Abraham that He would not destroy the city if at least ten righteous people were found in it; and while there wasn't even half that, God found one man and his family that were doing the best they could in a dark, dark place and He spared them. I don't think Jesus restricted Himself by who *would* come to salvation, but gave all of Himself so that everyone, every human being *could* come to salvation. A few years ago, you didn't even know Jesus; you didn't have a thought in the world about Him and now look at you. He loved you even before you knew Him and He would love you even if you never came to know Him just as much as He loves your parents. He does not love what they do or how they live and neither do you, and you shouldn't, but you should care about what happens to them. You should care about where they go when they die. That's love Kieri, that's the love that Jesus wants us to know and as much as I will miss you and I want so badly to keep you, I also know that like the people of Sodom and Gomorrah, your family needs someone to plead for them."

Two weeks later Kieri was back with her fathers and Riah. When she returned home, her Papa Scott was still in the hospital and Papa AJ acted as if nothing had happened.

~

Kieri stands up and returns to the bookcase where she saw the leather bound Bible resting obscurely on the shelf in her grandfather's office, unnoticed by everyone else, as no one but Kieri had any interest in reading it. While the edition was more mature in language, Kieri would make do with what she had. Papa AJ said she could make use of any book from the case and she was going to do just that. If Abraham could plead for hundreds of people he didn't even know for the sake of Lot and his family, Kieri could pray for the people she did know and plead intercession for the sake of her own family.

CHAPTER EIGHT

Scott is driving back to the house as Margo sits in the passenger seat with the shiny black box in her lap. She brought the makeshift urn with her from the house, explaining that her father had bought it years ago, full of some expensive cigars and as a joke; he said he wanted his ashes placed in it when he died. Margo figured there was no better place for him and why not fulfill his offhanded little suggestion at the same time. The box was a great deal larger than an average cigar box with a gold clasp on the front, matching gold hinges on the back, and Argo Stoddard's name engraved on a gold plate set on the very top.

"Thank you for bringing me into town, I normally drive myself but my vanity has been delaying me from getting to the doctor for a new prescription of eyeglasses and I didn't want to chance it; plus it gives us an opportunity to catch up." Margo adds as Scott forces a smile but keeps his eyes on the road ahead. Looking away only for a moment to catch Riah's reflection in the backseat as his daughter is playing with a doll Margo bought her in town.

"It's no problem. I'm surprised you didn't just have Tristan take you though." Scott suggests and Margo smirks.

"I take it you don't think too highly of him either? I can tell AJ can't stand him; or more accurately, he can't stand his age. Although to be honest, I think AJ's distaste for him is what drives me to see Tristan even more." Margo replies.

"Doesn't matter whether AJ or I like him; if he's what you want, you should be happy with him. I just figured after the way he was with you the other night, he'd be willing to drive you around anywhere." Scott explains and Margo begins to play with the latch on the box.

"Tristan isn't the errand running sort and honestly I wouldn't expect him to be. Tristan is the type of man that focuses solely on what he knows, to get what he wants. I don't think he's ever really done anything domestic or adult like, I don't even think he pumps his own gas, he certainly doesn't pay for it. Little realities like that ruin the fantasy of his life as one big party." Margo explains.

"I don't see why you bother with him then." Scott replies and Margo looks as if she is considering the comment.

"The same reason you bother with AJ, loneliness. Of course, in my case its loneliness and fear mixed with a little vanity. I know it's an overused cliché but being with Tristan, does make me feel a little less old. Besides, no one said anything about the old men that propositioned me when I was his age, and most of them were married." Margo replies and Scott frowns.

"I'm not with AJ because I'm lonely; I'm with him because I love him." Scott replies. Margo smiles as she continues to fidget with the box.

"Of course you are. Either way, thank you for helping me today. Now all that's left is to deal with the ashes. I don't want to keep them in the house. Maybe we can take them to a beach and dump them in the ocean?" Margo suggests as Scott turns into the roundabout driveway.

"Talk about an overused cliché." Scott replies as he parks on the side of the house with a view of the garden and the woods beyond. "I mean I know you and AJ say your father's death doesn't bother you and everything but this is still something you shouldn't just do to get it over with." Scott says. Margo sighs and looks down at the box.

"Yes I suppose I am just trying to put on a strong stance now that it is official. I know this is going to sound stupid but I think my dad was searching for immortality, or at least a way to cheat death. He thought his money could buy him more time and all those machines and medications really did was keep him conscious as he slowly deteriorated anyway, like being alive and aware while your body rots and decomposes. He said so many wild things toward the end that I hated even going to his room to bring him food. He would go on and on about how there was a curse on our family since the fire and he believed someone or something was after him to punish him for all of his sins. Which would explain why he was so scared of dying, I think he knew judgment was coming." Margo states as she stares out the window at the woods only a few yards away.

"It must've been horrible seeing him like that?" Scott suggests though he has no idea how she must have felt, as he did not know whether his own biological father was alive or dead and his mother died of a heart attack a year after Scott married AJ.

"I'd seen my grandfather go through some of the same things. Only not as bad as father's decline. You know granddad was very angry when he found out my dad was going to replace you? Of course, by then he was already upset about the addition of the islander boy that Oliver was supposed to fall in love with and Miranda becoming a trans-merperson, or whatever they called it on the show. He said Allan Teague was a pervert and went on and on about how Allan and my dad were sacrificing children for profit." Margo explains.

"For when you offer your gifts and make your sons pass through the fire, you defile yourselves with all your idols,"[2] Scott whispers and Margo looks at him curiously.

"Where is that from?" Margo asks but Scott becomes embarrassed and shakes his head.

"I don't know; it was probably from a movie I saw or something. Maybe your grandfather was one of the few who saw Teague for what he really was?" Scott adds to change the subject and Margo continues to stare at him but says nothing more on the issue of Allan Teague.

"Well, I don't mean to get rid of father's ashes unceremoniously. I just don't want them in the house for very long as we seem to have enough ghosts here." Margo explains. "Of course getting rid of this simple box of ashes won't resolve anything, so perhaps I should give it to that stupid statue Dad put out in the woods? It could be like an offering to appease Axel. Did AJ ever tell you about where that statue ended up?" Margo asks and Scott nods.

"He mentioned that your father was holding onto it after the fire. He said your dad still had hopes of fixing it and putting it in that theme park he wanted to open." Scott replies and Margo nods.

"The park that never was; I suspect after the park failed to manifest, Dad had other plans for that statue, though I have no idea what they were. I'm glad he never got that park off the ground and he was delusional then for not letting it go. I don't know why he had to put that thing out in the woods though." Margo says as she points toward the entrance of the woods. "If I had the nerve to go out there, I'd have it blown up into tiny

---

[2] EZEKIEL 20:31 (NKJV)

little pieces and finish what that fire couldn't." Margo replies without taking her eyes off the woods.

"Your father always believed I set that fire. He ruined my career over it." Scott says bitterly.

"Dad knew you didn't do it, he just wanted someone to blame. He didn't want to admit that the show ended because of his mistakes, so he blamed his own downfall on a fire and after some time he started to believe his own story of a curse. Toward the end of his life, I think my father started to believe Miranda was some sort of deity. I think he believed that he had offended her in some way because of the fire. However, that was just another example of how far gone he was mentally. The things he would say were so strange that I even started to miss the times when he was lucid and treated me horribly. His cruelty, I was used to and could handle but his insanity was another story that I thought would never end." Margo explains.

"Is that why you want us to move in? Because you think this house is haunted too?" Scott asks and Margo looks surprised.

"You're a lot smarter than I gave you credit for Scott. I don't know why AJ didn't just tell you the truth, but I'm glad you seem to be able to deduce things on your own. Yes, father's death is partly why I wanted you all to move in. I don't like being alone in this house and I want this place to be a real home, not a mortuary. Everything here was so cold, dark, and dead before you all arrived. I would leave the lights on all night, even when Tristan was here because his presence didn't help much and the darkness was starting to terrify me." Margo explains.

"Margo, you know there are no such things as ghosts and demons right?" Scott asks Margo, suddenly concerned about her mental state. AJ warned Scott that Margo wasn't quite right at times after all the abuse she suffered from their father and her mental breakdown over a decade earlier but Scott didn't imagine it was this bad. Maybe the seclusion in this house got to her or maybe she went through some of the same experiences as Scott when she was still making films? On the other hand, perhaps dementia was something inherited. Scott thinks to himself as Margo stares at him.

"Scotty, you should know better than anyone that ghosts and demons are very real and very hungry." Margo replies as she climbs out of the car and walks into the house carrying the heavy cigar box with two hands.

Later that night after everyone else has gone to bed, Scott pulls the children's Bible out from under the kitchen sink. He was going to throw it away the night before but feared Kieri might find it in the trash so he hid the book, after flipping through a few pages of it. His conversation with Margo that afternoon left Scott thinking about many things. When Scott and AJ first got together, before he ever came out about his sexuality to his father, AJ had full access to the Stoddard trust fund and could afford to do whatever he wanted, when he wanted. After Scott and AJ were married, Arthur banned AJ from ever returning to Stoddard Manor and cut him off completely from the trust. While Arthur Stoddard was an advocate for gay rights when it boosted viewership of his television show, he did not agree with his son reconnecting with Scott, whom he would always blame for the downfall of Stoddard Pictures. As Margo explained, Arthur would never hold himself or Allan Teague responsible for the decline in ratings or consider the fact that the content they were producing after *Oliver's* cancellation was nowhere near as good as the original

Oliver's Explorations, and for a cheesy puppet show, it was somehow, one of a kind.

Of course, Scott had no reason to complain, as he began producing music after coming to terms with the brutal fact that his acting career had reached its conclusion. It did not take long for him to realize how much he actually enjoyed music instead. Sadly, he lost all his clients after Kaila's death and the royalties he made previously from episode reruns were a small contribution to their rent after the condominium became too expensive. AJ's work as an influencer did not add much to the finances anymore either, as he lost most of his followers and endorsements over the past two years and was still trying to rebuild his brand. Even all those natural hair care products he promoted in his styling tutorials with the girls dropped him.

After their argument over dinner their first night in the manor, Scott realized how desperate AJ was to get back in the spotlight and possibly revive his family's dying name. AJ had not made a content video in a little over a year and he missed being on screen. When they were young AJ confessed that he was jealous of Scott because he got to be the star of his own show while AJ couldn't even get a small role from his father, even going so far as to audition as Scott's replacement as Oliver for the season that never got filmed. AJ's grandfather Argo once confessed to Scott that while he loved his grandson dearly, the talent bug never seemed to have a taste for him. Scott never considered himself a very good actor but someone saw something in him that led to his long run as Oliver and whatever it was, AJ was adamant that Kieri had it too, as many of AJ's old subscribers showered Kieri with praise for her onscreen demeanor and natural grace and beauty. Talent or not, Scott never wanted his daughters to know what he experienced as a child actor.

He was trying hard to remain resolute that he didn't want to do a reboot but every time AJ brought it up, the script and the idea continued to tempt him and the Stoddard's were just so desperate for a revival of their former glory that AJ would not let the matter go. While AJ swore that the girls would be safe, Scott had to consider how much he could rely on a promise from AJ.

With the kitchen light on, Scott opens the children's Bible and reads the inside flap in a whisper.

"To one precious young girl, may this give you strength for the battle and courage in the war; put on the whole armor of God and never forget on whose foundation you stand. Love Mrs. B." Who was Mrs. B. and why was she giving Kieri Bibles? Was she a teacher from Kieri's old school? Before her return home, Scott demanded that AJ transfer Kieri to another school as he blamed the careless administration at her old junior high for allowing some kind of cult to enter in and fill the student's minds with hate and judgment. AJ obliged since Kieri would be entering her first year of high school anyway. While suggesting that maybe the schools out this way near the manor did not allow such propaganda and might be better at deterring Kieri from joining another Jesus youth club or something like it. Of course, AJ only said that to help convince Scott to move up here, though AJ had yet to tell him that directly.

Scott opens the book on the marked page to find that Kieri was reading a story about three men who refused to bow to a statue the king had made.[3] The king was going to execute them by casting them into a large oven. Scott turns the page to find a color illustration of a giant oven and guards holding the three men by their clothes, getting ready to throw

---

[3] DANIEL 3 (NKJV)

them in the fire. This king was actually going to burn these men alive because they would not bow to a statue of God. Christians were maniacs even in the Bible, Scott thinks to himself.

If only his old friend Miranda were still around instead of this Axel character, then Scott would have someone to turn to for help. Of course, all Miranda's advice for Oliver was pretty ridiculous and only worked out in the end because they were following a script. Still he missed his time with the puppet mermaid but Scott somewhat understood the change. Axel was supposed to teach this new generation about the new world, inclusion and gender-discovery, a subject Kieri was missing the point of heavily and perhaps something *should* be done about it? Could Scott honestly go back to his roots of acting and play Oliver once again? Would the show even help Kieri realize the error of her ways? Did Scott really want to make a new life in Stoddard Manor? The bigger question was did he have a choice?

CHAPTER NINE

"Dad said that your father was a Christian and that's why he kicked Dad out for being gay, is that true?" Kieri asks Margo who smirks. The two of them are working in a flowerbed in the corner of the garden as Riah is nearby loading a toy dump truck with dirt and emptying it out all over again just to make a mess.

"I'm no theologian or anything but I'm pretty sure the god my father worshiped was not the Christian God. He had a strange faith that maybe only he understood, but he did use certain aspects of Christianity to condemn my brother. Of course, in my opinion I don't even think God has a problem with homosexuality anymore like people claim." Margo replies.

"The Bible says He does. Lots of chapters describe how God doesn't like lifestyles like that." Kieri explains in a low voice, as she grew accustom to doing whenever she spoke about God.

"Yes, but how current is the Bible nowadays? I mean there are ways around everything written in it. God said not to live in sexual immorality and that means don't have sex outside of marriage right? So what do people do? If they have been dating long enough, they just claim common law marriage or marry multiple times. Wasn't there a king in the Bible that had 1,000 wives?[4] I mean how much more immoral can you get sleeping with all those women and yet it was normalized and accepted because he called them his wives. It is also a question of what actually constitutes marriage. If two people love each other and they get married, is it still wrong that they are the same gender? Look at your fathers,

---

[4] 1 KINGS 11:3 (NKJV)

they're doing the best they can for you and your sister, and these two men are coming out of their own families that were so abusive and neglectful, *straight* parents that weren't very good at parenting. I don't believe that God would have a problem with two men raising children as long as they are doing it properly, so is homosexuality all that wrong anymore? Then take the Bible itself; it's a book, written by human beings with their own personal opinions, judgments and social commentary. You can't expect a book that large to not have personal thoughts somewhere." Margo explains.

"It's true the Bible is a book that was written by people, but those people were inspired by the Holy Spirit of God in what they wrote.[5] I mean I know there are good writers out there but I can't see anybody being able to write something that has so many meanings depending on where you are in life when you're reading it. That king you were talking about though, his name was Solomon, and I thought it was strange too about him having so many wives. His dad, King David had a lot of wives too and so did some other people in the Old Testament." Kieri replies and Margo looks hopeful.

"See what I mean, things that were common back then shouldn't be unusual now." Margo adds.

"Having a lot of wives was common back then but I don't think God ever gave them permission to do that." Kieri adds and Margo frowns.

"What do you mean? Weren't they men that followed God? If they were doing those things I would think that meant they got permission." Margo replies and Kieri shakes her head.

---

[5] 2 TIMOTHY 3:16-17 (NKJV)

"Not necessarily, I mean yeah, they were men who followed God, at least at some point in their lives, but it never says in the Bible that God told those men to marry so many women. The Bible never says that they asked, they just did it, maybe because it was normal for their culture. Until God did say, a person should have only one husband or one wife.[6] God doesn't even like divorce, and I read that it was only okay to do that if your husband or your wife cheated on you, or something to do with immorality and breaking the marital covenant.[7] The Bible isn't like a direct story of everyone doing the right thing. Some parts are about people doing what's wrong and I think that's in the Bible because if we don't see the consequences of doing the wrong things we won't know why it's wrong. Even King David, who loved God, had his own sins, which he had to seek forgiveness for and repent, because sometimes he let his flesh control him; but he wanted to do right and he wanted to honor God. David had many wives too and even more kids by those wives and many times his children hurt each other badly. One of his sons raped his own half-sister which led to one son killing the other in revenge and attempting to overthrow David as king.[8] As much as he loved God, David's children were lacking in their own relationships with the Lord. It could have been because they all had different mothers, so they competed with one another for David's attention and had no real love or compassion for each other. On the other hand, maybe they just felt disconnected because the shared blood of only their father wasn't enough. King Solomon, followed his wives and worshiped their foreign gods and idols and eventually he fell away from God and I don't think the end of his life was nearly as good as

---

[6] 1 CORINTHIANS 7:2 (NKJV)
[7] MATTHEW 5:31-32 (NKJV)
[8] 2 SAMUEL 13/ 2 SAMUEL 15-17 (NKJV)

the beginning.[9] God's word doesn't suddenly become invalid or outdated just because people stop following it or don't look into it at all. I don't think there are any loopholes like that when it comes to right and wrong." Kieri explains and Margo looks astounded.

"Well, does it bother you that you have two fathers? Do you think it's a sin?" Margo asks nervously. Kieri shrugs and looks at Riah.

"I do think it's a sin and it does bother me, but not *only* because of what the Bible says. Before I even learned about the Bible or God, I didn't like not having a mom. I hated that things would happen, like body issues and other stuff and I didn't have anyone to talk to about it. I mean I love my dads and they …I think they do the best they know how but sometimes our family just doesn't feel right and they fight with each other all the time, especially when they think no one notices. Papa AJ is always protesting something or finding something to be mad about and Papa Scott is always so sad. I guess I just thought that maybe all families were like us and then I found out they're not and I just couldn't un-see it." Kieri explains as she sets the flowers in the hole she dug and Riah approaches with her dump truck to fill the flowerbed with dirt.

"Kiwi!" Riah shouts as she empties dirt everywhere and runs away to get more.

"Thanks Riah!" Kieri calls back as she brushes away as much dirt as she can off the flower petals.

"I used to think every little girl needed a mother; someone to help her navigate growing up; someone to teach her to be strong and value herself. My own mother was good to me in her own way and I have nothing against her but sometimes I think about how she struggled on the inside. It

---

[9] 1 KINGS 11 (NKJV)

was as if she didn't always feel comfortable in her role as a mom and a wife. As she got older, she got very depressed when she realized that no amount of surgeries or injections or make-up would make her the beauty icon she once was. She immortalized herself in films but hated watching how those versions of her would never grow old. I think at some point she felt cheated." Margo laments as she empties another carton of flowers. "And then one day, after she put up with nearly two decades of my father's infidelities, he was the one who demanded a divorce. My father was already seeing AJ's mother Paige at the time and Paige was pregnant. By then my mother was so desperate to save her failed marriage she even started going to church, hoping that prayer would make things right for her. Her newfound religion did not last long though; as it was really just a fad for her or maybe a last resort that she never really believed would work. Either way, she was never quite the same when she finally accepted that my father would not take her back. I felt sorry for her before she died." Margo explains more to herself as she stares down into the flowerbed with sadness. After a moment, Margo forces a smile and changes the subject. "I'm sure puberty was an awkward conversation for you and your dads but do you really think overall that it's a bad thing? I mean, look at all they've done for you. You, Kaila, and Riah could have ended up in some terrible places, and you wouldn't have had nearly as many opportunities as you do now. You really believe that God would condemn two people for saving three children just because they are gay. I mean I always believed God looks at the heart of people. Your fathers do what they do with the best intentions." Margo explains as Riah approaches her this time with a truck full of dirt.

"Thank you sweetheart." Margo kisses Riah on the cheek and the little girl runs off excited to collect more dirt. Kieri stands up and stacks the empty flower trays to toss out later. She places the stack beside the garden bench.

"I used to think that too, about God looking at the heart and I never thought my dads were evil, I still don't, but sometimes we can let our hearts lead us in the wrong direction and tell ourselves that it's all God's will when it's not. The first time I ever read the Bible was when I was invited to this Bible study at school and I wasn't going to go at first because the Christian kids at school always seemed so inclusive. Anyway, these college kids ran the Bible study from a church in the area and they weren't mean, or stuck up at all. They were nice actually and they would bring us pizza and joke with us and sometimes we would play games, it was fun and I really didn't want to go home anymore, so I stayed. Then I went back the next week and the next week, until Tuesday afternoons became my favorite time. Even though what I was hearing went against everything I thought I knew, it just felt right. I never thought that I'd hear something that would make me question how my family lived. I was just joining a club because I didn't want to go home after school anymore. And whenever I was there listening to the Bible stories or answering questions or breaking down what I thought about the chapters we read that day, I just felt like I was at home, a real home. I know what my dads want and I know what they want me to say. They want me to compromise, to agree to disagree. My parents are okay with me following God as long as that doesn't change how I see them and that's a problem because God is going in a different direction than Papa AJ and Papa Scott." Kieri explains. Margo kneels in the flowerbed staring at Kieri with a sudden wave of compassion.

"I guess you have a very big decision to make and I can't say that I envy you or that I've ever been in your shoes before. I always just did everything my father told me to do or imitated whatever I saw my mother do and that hasn't always been healthy for me, but it was what I thought was right. So how does one follow God when the people she loves are not?" Margo asks and Kieri shrugs. Margo looks around the garden and realizes that Riah is no longer there. "Where's the little one?" Margo stands up to get a better view of the area but still cannot see Riah anywhere. Kieri immediately looks to the house but the backdoor leading to the kitchen has a catch over the handle that is too strong for Riah to lift and open on her own so she could not have gone back in that way.

"Maybe she went to the front of the house?" Kieri suggests as she leaves the garden and sprints to the front of the manor that leads to the driveway. Margo remains in the garden staring at the discarded toy dump truck on the path leading out the gate and into the woods. Margo inhales sharply and looks around to see if anyone else is nearby. There was no telling how far in the little girl had gone.

Margo enters the woods and reaches a small clearing only a few feet in. She can stick to the path to make it easier to find her way back to the garden but it was highly unlikely that a toddler would have done the same. Which way could Riah have gone? Margo decides to take the trail so far until she can hear something and only a few feet in there is a crunching noise behind her as if someone is following her. Margo stops and turns to see only the woods and the shrinking garden as she has gone further from the gate than she intended.

"Riah!" Margo shouts hoping the little girl will make some kind of noise and respond.

There is another crunch behind her and Margo turns again in the other direction this time facing deeper into the woods away from the house. There is no one there. That could not have been Riah's footsteps as it sounded like a much heavier shoe, like a man's boot. More crunching of dead leaves under foot as someone is coming toward Margo though she cannot see anyone. In a panic, Margo stumbles off the cobblestone path and heads deeper into the woods, running wildly to escape her pursuer. The footsteps quicken to keep pace and Margo looks back briefly to catch a glimpse of a large man in a gray jumpsuit marching after her. She cannot get a clear view of him behind her and run forward at the same time. Margo soon enters the deeper part of the woods, where there are more trees and less light as the foliage overhead is becoming thicker.

Margo looks back again but the man is gone and at the same time, she trips over a large root, her whole body hitting the ground hard. She can feel something pop in her wrist and the pain is almost blinding. Margo cries out but the only response is her echo. Not even the birds seem to live this deep in the woods. Margo rolls onto her back and tries to push her body into an upright position. As she struggles, she can hear the boots again. Margo freezes, hoping whoever is chasing her cannot see her on the ground. Of course, she is completely exposed and it is a silly hope that no one will see her there, but it is all she has. The boots come closer and Margo cradles her arm to her chest and shuts her eyes. Who would be out here on the property and where was Riah? She had to find that little girl, get her out of the woods, and get away from whoever was chasing her.

After a few moments of silence, Margo feels safe enough to sit up and look around. There is no one there, nothing but trees though the thin wisps of light breaking through the top play off the trunks and startle her a little. As much as she hates the woods, she knows she must find Riah first. Margo stands up slowly, being as tender as she can with her wrist and tries to regain her balance. She cannot remember what direction she came from when she stumbled off the path. Margo takes a step and winces as she realizes her knee is bleeding from the fall and her slacks torn with a growing bloodstain visible through the fabric. Taking one slow step after another Margo eventually reaches another clearing not far from where she fell. This space is larger than the first clearing at the entrance of the woods. She knows this place well enough. Margo gawks at the large figure looming over her from beneath the heavy tarp. She does not have to remove the covering to know what it is and even hidden, the figure gives her the chills. Margo begins to shake as she cautiously steps away from the statue. Her injured knee suddenly gives out and she drops to a kneeling position on the ground.

"Why are you haunting us? My father is dead and there is nothing here for you now. There is no one here to worship you." As Margo speaks, a breeze rustles the tarp at the base of the statue and Margo covers her mouth and begins to sob.

Margo was unconscious in the woods for over an hour before Scott finds her curled up on the ground near the statue she mentioned before. Scott only glances at the figure beneath the tarp before rushing over to Margo to see if she is okay. He can see streaks of mascara running down her face where she had been crying. As Scott picks her up off the ground, Tristan appears beside him acknowledging Margo only briefly before focusing in on the statue. As Scott heads back to the house with Margo in his arms, Tristan is pulling at the tarp to see underneath.

"Leave that alone!" AJ shouts as he appears with a rope in his hand, the other end of which Kieri is holding back in the garden as Riah stands beside her unaware of all the trouble her disappearance caused. When Kieri could not find Riah in the front of the house or a little ways back down the road beyond the driveway, she came back to the garden to find her Aunt Margo missing instead and Riah playing with her toy dump truck on the path entering the woods. Kieri brought Riah into the house thinking Margo had gone in as well to look for her. No one thought to look in the woods for Margo at first as Scott recalled that Margo did not like the area and there was really no reason for her to go in there. Until Tristan arrived claiming he and Margo had a date, which prompted Scott and AJ to look in the woods anyway and with a rope to find their way back as there was no telling how far she had gone or what route she had taken.

As Scott carries Margo back to the house, Tristan and AJ remain behind examining the covered statue.

"What is this?" Tristan asks and AJ adjusts the tarp so it is even all around the base of the statue.

"It's a gift my father had made for my grandfather for his birthday. It was supposed to be the centerpiece for the theme park, Oliver's Island." AJ explains as he begins walking back to the house while coiling the rope around his arm. He stops only to look back at Tristan who is still staring at the covered statue.

"So why is it way out here?" Tristan asks and AJ gives him a dirty look.

"That's none of your business!" AJ snaps at him without further explanation and Tristan frowns but follows AJ back to the house.

CHAPTER TEN

"No, no, no, do not come in here with that cough! I don't want you getting me sick again!" AJ commands from the kitchen as Scott approaches wearing his pajamas and robe with a large wad of tissues pressed against his nose.

"Well I wanted some soup and you weren't answering your phone." Scott replies from the doorway of the kitchen.

"Margo's still not feeling well and I was a little preoccupied trying to cook some comfort food for the both of you. Are you feeling any better at all?" AJ asks and Scott shrugs while leaning against the doorframe of the kitchen for support.

"Not really, my whole body still hurts and I can't go back to sleep." Scott replies.

"You know if you had listened to me and taken those supplements I bought you, you wouldn't be getting sick all the time." AJ replies and Scott pulls a bottle of pills from his robe pocket and shakes them in the air.

"I am taking them and they're not helping much." Scott replies as he yawns.

"Well they tend to work better if you take them before you get sick, not after." AJ replies as he empties a can of soup into a pot on the stove.

"On the rare occasions when I'm feeling better, the last thing on my mind is to take a supplement to stay that way. Besides this stuff is all snake oil anyway." Scott replies as he pulls a chair out of the dining room so he can sit in the doorway of the kitchen.

"Those are vitamins your body is lacking because you don't eat right. Snake oil is that tap water my father used to drink because he thought it was a cure all to his ailments and would keep him alive forever." AJ's reply makes Scott laugh and then cough uncontrollably. "I swear you have the weakest immune system, you must've been a cesarean baby." AJ says as he prepares a bowl and crackers for the soup. Scott frowns and AJ notices. "Don't look at me like that, it's a well-known fact that cesarean born babies come out missing key nutrients to their health and always get sick." AJ explains in his familiar know-it-all tone and Scott shakes his head.

"Do not be wise in your own eyes but fear the Lord and depart from evil and it will be health to your flesh and strength to your bones."[10] Scott mumbles to himself without thinking. AJ looks at him quizzically as he is stirring the pot of soup on the stove.

"What did you say?" AJ asks and Scott shakes his head.

"Nothing, it's not important. Hey, do you remember someone named Mrs. B. that worked at Kieri's old school? Maybe a counselor or someone she mentioned?" Scott asks, changing the subject. The Bible he took from Kieri remained hidden under the sink, as he was too distracted the past few days to throw it out. With Margo falling in the woods and hurting herself along with Scott getting sick, that left AJ to care for everyone alone. AJ pours the soup into the bowl and places everything on a standing tray, which he sets in front of Scott who is still sitting in the hallway outside the kitchen. AJ tries to remember anyone named Mrs. B. but eventually shakes his head.

---

[10] PROVERBS 3:7-8 (NKJV)

"I don't remember a Mrs. B. from her school, but I didn't spend too much time getting to know the admin there. The teachers and staff were so pretentious, but I guess that was what we were paying for at the time. Of course, we were not on the best of terms after I sued them either. I mean, yeah they have their degrees for this or that, but they didn't know much about respecting people. I know they were so jealous of me too when they found out I was an influencer making enough money to send our daughters to that school in the first place, as if it's a demeaning profession or something. They just hated that the girls came from a family who could afford the tuition." AJ replies, still bitter about when he had to pull Kieri from the private school when the family could no longer afford the tuition after Kaila's death. Scott frowns over his bowl of soup.

"Not to make it a thing but I'm sure my own income contributed to their tuition just a little." Scott replies sarcastically and AJ rolls his eyes before returning to the cookbook he has propped up on the stove.

"Poor Margo is still in a lot of pain and she's been acting really strange since that fall in the woods. I tried to ask her why she was even out there since she's so terrified of that place but she just got emotional and acted as if she couldn't talk about it. I know she's dealt with a lot of depression over the years because of our father, which I think turned into some self-esteem issues, both of which would explain why Tristan is around, though I'm sure it won't last much longer. Add that to her repressed anger toward our father and maybe even a little shock at seeing Dad in that cigar box and I think the combination really got to her the other day. I always hated the way my father used to walk all over her and bully her, I thought she'd be happy to see him reduced to ashes but I definitely wasn't expecting her to react this way." AJ explains and Scott shrugs over his soup.

"I know your dad was a cruel man, I mean even I had my own reasons for not liking him, but you had some love for him, didn't you?" Scott asks and AJ frowns at him.

"Yeah I had about as much love for him as you had for your mother." AJ quips and Scott does not say anymore as AJ returns to his cookbook looking for something good to make, but stops when he suddenly remembers something.

"Hey did you say, Mrs. B? I do remember someone with that name." AJ says and Scott looks up.

"Who is she? How does Kieri know her?" Scott asks and AJ shrugs.

"Well I'm pretty sure the woman who ran the group home you sent Kieri to was a Mrs. B. I remember seeing the names Mr. and Mrs. Braeger on all this different paperwork when I was filing to get Kieri back. What made you even think of her? Did someone call here?" The potential answer to who Mrs. B. is throws Scott off a little and he does not respond to AJ right away.

"Scotty, why were you asking about Mrs. B?" AJ asks again and Scott looks at him.

"Um, no reason, the name just popped into my head and I figured it was someone I must've met through Kieri; just a name that came to mind." Scott explains and AJ nods before settling on a recipe from the book.

"That is strange that she was just randomly on your mind." AJ says and Scott slouches in his chair knowing where AJ is going with this.

"AJ give it a rest it was just a name that came to me." Scott argues as he finishes his soup and AJ rests a hand on his hip defensively.

"I'm sure you'd like to see it that way but I don't believe in coincidences like that. I just think that maybe it wasn't random that you were thinking of this woman Mrs. B. because she ran the home Kieri spent months in and your conscience is telling you to apologize to her!" AJ snaps back and Scott remains silent. "I'm tired of my family wandering around this house like ghosts or something. You two never used to be so awkward around each other this way and when you do talk, it's … different, like you don't know each other and that's not a family. I messed up, you messed up and Kieri messed up; why can't we all just move on from it!" AJ asks in frustration.

"You didn't actually think bringing us up here was going to just fix all our family problems did you? I know reconciliation isn't the only reason we're here. We can't even afford the rent on that slum apartment anymore and now you want us to rebuild an entire estate! What happens when it comes time to pay taxes on this place? You think my meager little royalties or the remains of your trust fund will cover that! We are broke AJ and you are trying to run away from our problems again! So stop complaining about Kieri and me as if you don't have your own awkward elephants in the room." Scott counters.

"I came out here to help my family; Margo didn't want to be alone up here and I see no reason why she should be! I don't expect everything to just fall into place for us, but the very least you can do, is apologize to Kieri. She deserves to hear her father admit he made a mistake and you did make a mistake whether you want to admit it or not; and speaking of us being broke, you will admit that we are having financial troubles but you won't do the one thing that could help us. How does that make sense to complain about the problem but do nothing when the solution is right in your hands?" AJ asks.

"Doing a reboot of a stupid puppet show is not the solution to our problems. At best those checks will cover a few minor things but nothing in television is promised long term. Without a steady income we'll just pour money into restoring this place just to lose it a year from now or five years from now or ten years from now." Scott explains but AJ is not having it.

"I am not giving up this home without a fight! It is my birthright! This house, this property is all that is left of my family's legacy and I will do anything in my power to save it! I never said doing the reboot was a long-term thing. I'm only considering what could be the beginning of Kieri and Riah's careers?" AJ argues.

"Come on AJ you sound just like my mother. You know you never even asked them if they wanted to do this show. You just told Kieri about it as if it was supposed to be the best news she ever heard. You don't care about what shoving a camera in our kid's faces does to them. Parents like you never do." Scott replies.

"Oh, so now I'm a bad parent because I want to encourage our kids in their talents?" AJ asks with hostility but Scott does not back down.

"I never said that. I never said that you don't care about our kids or that you don't love them. I said you don't care about what filming them all the time does to them. I mean what are you doing filming hair tutorials with the girls and coming out with your own line of black hair care products. You had no business doing any of that, trying to market our daughter's race. And what about Kaila and you documenting her transitioning, those things are private and personal, Kyrie didn't need that." Scott says but AJ cuts him off.

"Don't use her dead name, it's disrespectful. Her name was and is Kaila." AJ says sharply and Scott stares at him.

"*That's* disrespectful? Okay, well what about your Riah videos?" Scott asks.

"What about them? People love those videos." AJ replies, remembering fondly his time filming their youngest daughter.

"I'm sure you like to think that all the positive comments made it real wholesome. I guess you never looked at the views on some of your Riah videos compared to others?" Scott asks and AJ stands defiantly.

"What exactly are you getting at Scott?" AJ asks and Scott cannot bring himself to answer.

"What is that supposed to mean Scott?" AJ asks again, this time with more hostility. Without another word, Scott stands up and leaves the room, his empty chair and food tray still blocking the kitchen doorway.

CHAPTER ELEVEN

"You don't have to stay up here with me all day; I'm sure you want to get out and go to a party or something. I'll be perfectly fine by myself." Margo explains to Tristan as he is sitting on the edge of her bed watching television and looking like a grounded teenager. Startled, Tristan looks at Margo who is sitting by her bedroom window watching the sunset.

"Why don't we go out together? We haven't been on a decent date in over a week. In fact, I've barely been able to see you since your family arrived." Tristan replies a little sourly and Margo smiles. She knows his distaste for her family's presence is solely on the fact that he is no longer the center of her attention and she has no time to keep him occupied or interested with shopping trips and expensive nights out.

"You make it sound like I've been completely ignoring you. You know you're welcome at the house anytime; you could even move in if you wanted to?" Margo suggests and Tristan frowns at her.

"Your brother doesn't like me. You should have seen the look he gave me when I got here today. There is no way he would let me move in." Tristan replies.

"AJ doesn't have a say on who lives here and who doesn't; this is my house, left to me by my father as his eldest child and if you want to live here you can." Margo explains authoritatively. In actuality she only invited Tristan to move in when they first met because she could not stand being alone at night in the house after her father died. Tristan spent a few nights over but not as a routine; and his presence did not help much to ease her fears. However, she did appreciate the times he managed to keep her out of the house completely some nights until AJ and Scott's arrival.

Now she really had no need for Tristan to move in at all, but out of compassion for a struggling actor like him, the offer was still on the table. Margo is no fool, she knows Tristan is only with her for what he can get, whether he expects Stoddard Pictures to bounce back or he is just hanging around until Margo cannot cover his expenses anymore, Tristan is only there to profit himself. Of course, she did not blame him for it as she did the same thing decades ago when she was his age, with men even older than she is now.

"No it's alright; I don't want to leave you alone. I'd rather stay here with you and keep you company." Tristan replies in defeat and Margo cannot help but appreciate little moments like these when he can seem genuine and caring. Perhaps he was a better actor than she gave him credit for; or maybe he was drawing from his real compassion toward his mother, to whom he would often compare Margo?

"If you're worried about me because of what happened in the woods, I'm absolutely fine now. It was days ago and I'm over it." Margo explains, while trying her best to hide her anxiety. Since her fall in the woods, Margo refused to come out of her room and spent most of her time there trying to understand what she had seen in the woods and why that statue frightened her so much.

"How are you over it? You hurt your wrist and your knee pretty badly and since then you haven't come out of this room, you call that being over it?" Tristan snaps; possibly annoyed by the fact that he did not sign up for any real life issues in their relationship.

"Actually I call it recovering and I'll be downstairs tomorrow making breakfast for my family, I'm including you as well when I say *family* because that's what you are to me now. God might not consider us or my brother and his husband a couple … but I think the devil does and that's good enough for me." Margo says, while forcing herself to laugh but even she cannot find that funny deep down. Tristan gives her a curious look.

"Where did that come from? Since when do you believe in God and the devil? Have you been hiding a little religion from me lately?" Tristan asks sarcastically and Margo frowns.

"I've always believed in God and I love Him in my own way and I have my own relationship with Him. I even have my mother's old Bible around here somewhere. I may not be as devout as my niece but I still believe in God and plan to go to heaven." Margo says confidently though lately she was not so sure about her salvation on the inside. Her conversation with Kieri in the garden left her with a few questions about her past and present decisions in life.

"Kieri's a Christian? That must be awkward for your brother." Tristan replies with a smirk. "Well, don't bother trying to sell any of that my way. God has nothing for me and I'm offering nothing to Him." Tristan replies and Margo looks at him in surprise.

"What are you an atheist?" Margo asks and Tristan shrugs.

"If that's the term you want to use. I consider myself more of a realist. With the exception of you, anyone I have ever met who believes in God seems a little off. It's foolish to put all your trust in something or someone that has never done anything to earn that trust." Tristan explains and his comment surprises Margo.

"I didn't realize you felt so strongly about all this." Margo says and Tristan shrugs again.

"Only when it's brought up, otherwise I don't really care one way or the other what a person believes in. Some of us survive on delusion while others, like me, know what we have and learn to use it to our advantage."

Tristan explains and Margo nods, remembering a time when she would have agreed with him.

"I can see your point, but maybe I only bring up God and the devil now because Kieri got me thinking about how I used what I had for my career and what it cost me overall. We were talking out in the garden the day I fell and we got on the subjects of immorality and sin and she told me she thought the way her fathers were living was wrong." Margo shares and Tristan holds his hands up as if Kieri's feelings prove his point.

"You see what I mean about religion? Someone is always in your face trying to get you to believe what he or she believes and what he or she believes is all nonsense. I mean I don't know this girl's life story or anything but it seems like your brother and his husband give her whatever she wants. The simple fact that they brought her into their home and raised her as their own should be enough for her to have a little gratitude. She could've ended up much worse off so what is she complaining about?" Tristan asks in frustration.

"I wondered that too at first, until she explained why she thought that way about her fathers. She told me it bothered her that she didn't have a mother to run to about private things and how it always felt off in her family, even before she started following God. Of course I had a mother around but there were so many things she never taught me, never warned me about, so I can only partially understand where Kieri is coming from. AJ and Scott are no perfect couple as much as they try to seem like they are on camera, but honestly, who is? So maybe Kieri is judging them a little too harshly, but she's a sweet girl and I don't think she tries to bully religion on her parents, at least, not anymore. Don't tell anyone I told you, but a while back, Scott sent Kieri to a foster home. It was after Kaila died; the one I told you about, Kieri's twin. Right after the funeral AJ fled to parts unknown with whomever he was messing around with at the time, before making his way here when our dad was still alive. If there was one trait my brother inherited from father it was his infidelity. A few weeks after AJ arrived, crying for attention and financial help, Scott called here looking for him. He told my brother that Kieri intended to be baptized at school in some Bible study she joined and a few days later she was ranting at Scott about how he and AJ were going to hell and she was scared that her twin was already there. Scott was furious, after everything they had done for her, and for her to say that to him was just too much, so he packed her bags and sent her away. This was months before he was able to track AJ here and Kieri had been in a group home that entire time. By then Scott was only looking for AJ to let him know that he couldn't hold on to things anymore or something like that and was going to put himself in the hospital, he'd been committed before so it was nothing new for Scott. AJ flew back home to take care of Riah, who wasn't even walking at the time. Scott had a full on emotional breakdown; the loss of two of his children just destroyed him." Margo adds and Tristan looks in shock.

"If they script an episode like that on the *Oliver* reboot, I might just watch the show." Tristan replies.

"Oh my brother would never do a thing like that because it would ruin the image of happy gay couples everywhere. Death and other tragedies happen often enough in my family and I'm beginning to think perhaps my father was right and we are cursed. Anyway, even though all that was some time ago, it looks like the situation is still a little raw with them all, so you can see why it is important that I help them now. I don't mean to be a homebody all of sudden, but my brother needs me." Margo explains as Tristan considers everything.

"So what exactly happened to Kieri's twin? I know you said she killed herself but why?" Tristan asks and Margo rests her back against the cool glass of the window.

"Well like I told you, she was born a male, Kyrie was her real name, AJ calls it her dead name so don't say it out loud in front of him. She began to transition when she was about ten I think and that's when she changed her name to Kaila and started filming and documenting everything on AJ's channel. I think she was even growing breasts at one point from some kind of hormone therapy. My brother's plan was to have Kaila go through puberty alongside Kieri, so they could be identical twins. I'm not saying this to sound cruel or to speak ill of the dead but honestly that girl just didn't look right to me at all. I mean the drugs and the operations and everything else just made it that much more obvious what she used to be and deformed her in such a way that she really didn't look like a girl or a boy anymore. She kept saying she felt beautiful but I don't know. One day when she was about twelve or thirteen, while she was taking all these new medications, she got hold of Scott's anti-depressants, went to sleep in the bathtub, and never woke up. At the time, Kaila was out of school for a few weeks and was supposed to be babysitting Riah that day. Poor Kieri came home to find the little one in her crib screaming and crying and when she went into the bathroom, there was Kaila." Margo explains. Tristan listens intently as he takes a cigarette from the box on Margo's dresser and lights it for himself. His expression is one of shock and confusion.

"Well why do they say she killed herself, maybe it was an accident?" Tristan suggests.

"Darling, I wasn't even there and I know she did what she did intentionally, and so does Scott and my brother, though AJ will never say it out loud." Margo replies coolly.

"But why would she do something like that to herself if she was happy about the transition?" Tristan asks in honest confusion and Margo stares at him.

"I would assume she did it because she *wasn't* happy about the transition. Maybe she regretted it and by then everything had gone too far? You should know by now that just because someone smiles on camera, it doesn't mean they are actually happy." Margo explains.

"Well, maybe if she had gotten some kind of help or support she'd still be alive? Or more likely Kieri was bullying her about God and pushed her to it?" Tristan suggests but Margo cuts him off.

"Kieri wasn't a Christian when Kaila died and you have no right trying to blame her for what happened! That poor girl had the bad luck of finding her twin dead in a bathtub, so don't make her out to be some kind of villain here. This is one instance where people like you who don't believe in God have no business blaming God or people who believe in Him, for someone else's choices! Besides, how much more support did she need if her school was already accommodating the change by allowing a biological boy to use the girl's restroom? Nearly everyone was calling her Kaila and her fathers were going on as if nothing was off, so I don't think the issue was lack of support. Did the whole world need to move to validate what she was doing and why did she even need validation to do it? Perhaps because it felt wrong, no matter how many people said it was right. I truly believe that Kaila reached a point where she regretted it, and by then she couldn't go back to the way she was before. The damage was done and asking for help takes admitting that you actually need it." Margo replies.

"I still don't understand why she didn't just admit she wasn't happy. Or ask for help." Tristan suggests, though he seems less sure of his opinions now. Margo turns away from him to look out the window again.

"If you were promoting something so controversial for years and clapping back at everyone who said you were making a mistake, would you be so quick to admit to those same people that you had indeed made a mistake and there was no going back now? No, you would keep doing the wrong thing until it turns out right and when it doesn't you'd cash out early and hope for the best on the other side. Everyone has regrets, but not everyone admits to them." Margo replies and Tristan slides onto the bed to stretch out as he is talking to her.

"I don't have any regrets." Tristan states directly and Margo frowns at him.

"Perhaps you're the exception? Maybe you just haven't lived long enough for your demons to catch up to you. I bet if you ever reach my age you'll have a few and then maybe you'll have a slightly different view of God and the devil." Margo replies and Tristan raises an eyebrow at her.

"I doubt it. And I thought you said you weren't as extreme as your niece when it came to God?" Tristan asks.

"I'm not, I mean, I believe in God and I love Him, but some things are more complicated than others. I've never stolen anything, or killed anyone, I'm charitable and I think I'm a good person but when Kieri and I were talking she brought up something interesting about immorality and marriage and it made me think of my ex-husband. I didn't know what I was doing when I married him. I was nearing 40 and my career was … not where I wanted it to be, so marriage just seemed like the next best thing. The problem was that I didn't love him and I think he actually loved me and he wanted so much of me that I wasn't willing to give. Anyway, Kieri mentioned something about people not asking God who they should marry and it really stuck with me. My intention was to use my ex-husband, and I didn't really feel guilty about it until now. I've never tried talking to God about anything before I do it; I mean I don't even pray." Margo's voice cracks, as she seems near to tears. She motions to the cigarette pack and Tristan lights one and passes it to her.

"You wouldn't have heard much other than your own thoughts if you did pray. If everyone in the world waited on God to tell them who to marry and how to go about anything in their own lives, either no one would do anything because they didn't hear anything or the world would still be in chaos because everyone would just do what they want and claim it was God's will. And you make it sound like you would have been better off not marrying Bob or Bill or whatever his name is." Tristan replies a little sharply.

"His name is Bob, Bob Hensley; I was the only one who ever called him Robert." Margo replies fondly as she blows smoke out the open window into the night air. "Imagine, out of all the men I ever knew, he was the kindest to me and I was the cruelest to him. So I guess I do regret marrying him because I hurt him, I used him and I learned too late that alimony isn't the most important thing in life and while it's nice, sometimes I think I'd rather have love instead, or maybe both? I don't really know." Margo replies as she tries to brush off the thoughts entirely though she cannot seem to shake the seed that Kieri planted in her mind.

"I love you." Tristan says with a smile.

"Considering how much of a financial benefit I am to you, I almost feel like I'm getting my money's worth when you say that." Margo replies and Tristan frowns.

"That's not funny, I'm not a hustler; and I do love you and I would still love you if you had nothing at all. You got married because you thought it was the right thing to do and it didn't work out so you got a divorce, if that's a sin then I guess neither one of us is going to heaven." Tristan replies.

"It's more than that though. When I thought about Robert and my marriage, I started to think about other things in my life. Decisions I made that might have been different if I had listened to God first, if I had asked Him which direction to take. Like my career, I never considered God at all in that area of my life. I might have convinced myself it was just a movie or just a nude scene, or just a sex scene in the moment; but where I am in life now, I can't say that I'd ever done anything that made me proud. So if I've never done any work *I* was proud of, could I believe that I'd done anything God was proud of me for doing?" Margo asks, visibly upset now.

"Why does it matter if He is proud of you or not? You think that if there were a God, He would be worried about what you're doing. It's one thing to believe in Him on certain occasions, you can believe in God and have a life too. It's another thing to put God into every aspect of your life. It's unnecessary." Tristan replies.

"What's unnecessary is how I've lived my life and all the stupid decisions I've made. When I was young I wanted to be famous, I wanted to be glamorous like my mother and make lots of money and be on screens all over the world. Now after nearly two decades of sleeping with producers, taking my clothes off for auditions, and exploiting myself and pretending it was female empowerment, what do I have to show for it, but a string of terrible, straight-to-video horror films. The most notable being a dumpster fire of a movie called Blood Dip, about a bunch of sorority girls that rent a cabin in the woods for no other reason than to be killed by a masked maniac in a jumpsuit. My character was a nameless sorority sister that takes a skinny dip alone at night, and then runs through the woods completely naked from the killer who eventually stabs her to death and leaves her dead body for the animals, like trash! That is what all my characters were and I sold myself for that? I took my clothes off for that! I prostituted myself for that! For years, I told myself if I just acted as if I was proud of my career, all the horror conventions, the fan-bases, and the nostalgia would make it worth it! The truth is that none of that lasts and now all I have left are the demons that followed me home. It's hitting me all at once now that there might have been a better way to life and my career. I mean everything I ever filmed seemed to glamorize and romanticize horrible and ungodly things, making perversity look cool somehow. Who knows what was encouraged in a person from the trash I made? And whether I like it or not I'm responsible for that and I can't really be happy in life now knowing that I missed out on an opportunity to do things the right way, if there even was a right way in that line of work? I could've been happy, really and truly happy, if I hadn't been offering myself up to the gods of entertainment!" Margo turns away in embarrassment over her outburst and stares out the window into the growing darkness. She can still see Tristan's reflection through the glass as he looks at her as if she has lost her mind.

"Margo, everyone gets old, I mean even I know I'll get old too. Sometimes we just reach a point in our lives when the industry doesn't need us anymore. And it's not like you're starving so all your work wasn't for nothing." Tristan tries to explain and Margo faces him.

"This isn't about ageism! It's not even about money, it's about waste; don't you understand that? Of course you don't. You are at your peak in life, living off a lonely old woman, bouncing from party to party, girl to girl, maybe even girl to guy for all I know. You won't see the reality of things until you get too old to be living so shiftlessly. You are just like AJ; you don't see the cost of things. He's trying to revive a show that ruined many lives. He's trying to bring back something that started off good but just became this warped version of a children's show; it became something that perverted what few good things were left in the world." Margo replies.

"I'm not trying to live off of you and I don't bounce around from person to person or party to party." Tristan replies. "I do care about you, I love you, *in my own way,* but I also love living in the moment and just because I'm not the type of person who lives their life based off of some invisible entity's rules doesn't mean I'm evil or bad and just because you claim to believe in God doesn't make you good. It doesn't make Kieri or anyone else good either. What if there is nothing on the other side of death and I waste my life being a shut-in or a homebody trying to get into a heaven that doesn't even exist? So just like you, I do what I do to get what I want and I am not ashamed of that. Your brother is trying to bring something back that could profit you and him; a return to the industry you said used you, except now you could be coming back on your own terms. You should be helping him, not trying to condemn him for it." Tristan replies, clearly angry with Margo for her assumption of his character. He knew he was not faithful to her because they never agreed in the beginning that he needed to be and she had no right to throw it in his face now.

"There are no personal terms when it comes to acting. One way or another someone owns you when you get in front of that camera, because selling yourself was the only way to *get* in front of that camera. My grandfather thought he could make wholesome television; he thought he could do things on his own terms and you see how that turned out. My father and my grandfather, both supposedly suffered from dementia; where my father was violent, confused and angry, my grandfather was still sweet and kind. He had moments of what I thought was confusion back then but I am starting to realize now with what clarity Granddad was seeing things. He said some very strange and out of character things before he died but it was almost as if he could see into the future when he started to lose perspective on the present. My grandfather told my father that Dad was selling the souls of children. That with the changes my dad was making to *Oliver's Explorations*, he was compromising the futures of fans everywhere, teaching little ones evil and destructive things. He said that Dad would pay for his idolatry and he did. You say you don't want to waste your life in case heaven doesn't exist; my father lived the same way and he found out too late that heaven is real and so is hell. A whole lifetime of doing what he wanted, when he wanted at the cost of others and by the end, he was so senile he was calling me by my mother's name and apologizing for all the terrible things he'd done to her. His apologies were decades too late and she couldn't hear them from wherever she is now. He was so afraid in the end that he begged me not to cut the lights off at night because that was when he saw the monsters he created and he believed they would get him when there was no light left to protect him.

He said he was afraid of dying in darkness because that's when *they* would catch up to him and he'd be punished for his sins." Margo explains.

"I'm not a doctor but it sounds like that's just what happens when a person is sick; none of that means that heaven or hell exists. Dementia affects a lot of people and at least now you know they're not suffering anymore" Tristan replies in a comforting tone.

"I'm not positive that my father isn't still suffering somewhere. Moreover, I said my father and grandfather *supposedly* had dementia. My grandfather may have been off at times but he knew what he was saying back then. My father on the other hand suffered torment for his sins and crimes. For doing what he did and knowing it was wrong but he still did it anyway because he thought he would never be punished for it or perhaps he loved the profit of man more than he feared the wrath of God? Either way, what my brother is trying to bring back is wrong. It was toxic for anyone back then and it is just as toxic for everyone now. And while I don't believe dementia is inherited, I'm terrified that perhaps sins and demons are." Margo explains and Tristan sighs.

"If you say so Margo." Tristan mumbles before returning his attention to the television, though Margo's comments are unsettling to him.

"You say you love me in your own way but I wonder, if dementia is inherited, would you sacrifice living in the moment to live day to day to take care of me? Would you take doing what you want to get what you want and exchange it for doing what you need to do to give me what *I* need?" Margo asks and Tristan stares at the television, saying nothing and refusing to look at her. "Of course you wouldn't; but then again, as much as I claim to love God, I wouldn't sacrifice what I thought I wanted for what God wanted for me, so how could I expect anything from you?"

Margo replies and the two remain in awkward silence with the drone of the television in the background.

CHAPTER TWELVE

"I am not ashamed we're not the same! I love our differences they make us shine! What's good for me is good for me, what's good for you is good for you! As long as we do what just makes us happy!" Oliver and Miranda finish the song in unison as they sit together on the beach. At least what looks like the beach on the television screen as Young Scotty watches himself on the monitor in Arthur Stoddard's office. It took all the courage Scotty could muster to come up here to tell Arthur … Mr. Stoddard what was going on and immediately the older man brushed Scotty off to make a phone call in one of the other offices.

The episode Scotty was watching was filmed a few days earlier and while it looked complete on screen Scotty knew how fake it was and the experience ruined television for him. If only Grayson had come with him. Scotty was so mad that he had to do this alone and Grayson was the one who convinced Scotty to say something yet he was not even here and Scotty was sure that was why Mr. Stoddard did not believe his confession about Allan Teague.

As young Scotty watches the credits scroll on the screen, Arthur returns and begins to snap in Scotty's face.

"Hey, wake up! I step out for two minutes and you turn into a zombie." Arthur accuses as he sits down at his large desk, which causes Scotty to sink further into his own much smaller chair on the other side, from embarrassment. Arthur and Scotty stare at each other in awkward silence before Arthur presses his fingertips together under his chin as if he is deciding on something.

"Listen, I've known Allan for a long time now, and what you're saying could cost him his job, his credibility, not to mention his freedom. You need to know that making accusations like this is a big deal." Arthur replies, a little too calm for the situation and Scotty shrinks further into the chair.

"It's all true; just ask Grayson, it's been happening to him too." Scotty replies as he looks down in shame and Arthur frowns.

"And yet he isn't here with you now." Arthur says.

"I asked him to come with me but he was scared. He said he didn't want anything to happen to his role on the show now that he and his parents have just moved into a new house." Scotty replies, and Arthur nods, clearly not believing the young man's story.

"Yeah okay, I'm sure that's what it is. Well the only way to figure this out is to call Teague up here." Arthur replies as he picks up the phone.

"No, don't do that!" Scotty shouts, panicking and Arthur sets the phone down.

"Scott I'm not going to take just your word for this. It sounds like you are misinterpreting all of this. Besides, Allan has a right to defend himself here." Arthur lifts the phone again when there is a knock at the door. "Come in!" Arthur shouts and Allan Teague enters the office, faking a look of surprise at seeing Scotty there.

"I was just about to call you." Arthur says and Allan looks confused.

"Is something wrong?" Allan asks Arthur while staring at Scotty.

"Well, actually we do have a bit of an issue here. Scott has just told me something pretty alarming and I need you to clear all this up and explain to him that what's done in rehearsal is just that, a rehearsal for the show and that it's not real. I think maybe Scott has been a little uncomfortable with your methods." Arthur explains with disinterest as he conveniently focuses on some paperwork on his desk as Allan stares at Scotty.

"I'm sorry Scotty. I wish you had come to me directly if you were feeling uncomfortable about the story or any of the scenes we were rehearsing. In that interview with the magazine, you said you were on board with it and everything. You said you were excited about being a part of diversity. So what happened?" Teague asks as he reaches for Scotty's shoulder but the young man darts out of the chair and stands up.

"Don't touch me!" Scotty shouts and Arthur looks appalled while Allan fakes concern.

"Hey, take it easy young man! Why don't you calm down and stop all that shouting!" Arthur orders Scotty and Teague raises his hands submissively.

"I'm sorry Art that was my fault. You just said he was uncomfortable about something and I had no right to make it worse." Teague admits with a smile.

"No, it's not your fault at all. He's got no right to be getting hysterical like that and he knows it." Arthur replies in Allan's defense before addressing Scotty directly. "And you, young man, need to take a seat. You save all that dramatics for the audience. Now Allan is here trying to explain to you that you are taking things out of context and you were on board for the storyline when it got you an interview or two but now you're not, which is giving me some second thoughts about you. Maybe Oliver needs to be recast with an actor that's less homophobic and more dedicated to doing his job!" Arthur snaps and Scotty fights back tears.

"This isn't about the storyline, what he was doing had nothing to do with the storyline." Scotty replies and Arthur goes red.

"I told you accusations like that are dangerous. If you don't want to do your job any more, I see no reason to renew your contract." Arthur replies and Allan tries to speak up on Scotty's behalf.

"Oh, come on Art, the kid is just going through some things. I'm sure there is a reason for all of this and no one has to get fired." Allan explains as if trying to calm the situation, although he still has a grin on his face.

"I think you owe Allan an apology, because he's being real patient with you considering what you're trying to accuse him of and the fact that you have no witnesses, including Grayson, says a lot about who is telling the truth here." Arthur says to Scotty who is looking down at the floor as the room begins to tilt slightly.

"Really that's not necessary Arthur, my feelings aren't hurt here; I mean I learned how to have thick skin a long time ago. We can just pretend this whole thing never happened." Allan suggests again but Arthur refuses.

"No, I told him to apologize to you and he's going to do it. Apologize to him Scott." Arthur commands Scotty calmly. Scotty can feel his heart beating rapidly in his chest and he shakes his head slowly but says nothing.

"Okay, well then that's that. You don't want to be here anymore and we don't want you here anymore. You'll finish out the season and that's it; now go home." Arthur says and Scotty crosses the room in silence, avoiding Allan's fake sympathetic gaze.

When young Scotty steps out of the office, he emerges on the beach on a bright sunny day as an adult. Scott looks back and instead of Arthur's office, there is a cluster of fruit trees and fake little huts off in the distance behind him. When Scott turns around again, the ocean is in front of him and there is Axel with a large group of children again. The children sit at Axel's feet staring up at the puppet, which is alarmingly larger now, almost the size of a human adult, and still sitting on the rock, moving independently of a puppeteer. Scott crosses the beach in anger as he recalls that day in Arthur's office and what a fool he had been and what his so-called bravery had cost him.

As Scott approaches the group, he can see that Axel is holding a large book in their hands and as Scott closes in the distance, he can see the bright illustrations on the cover of the children's Bible he took from Kieri. Axel eyes Scott curiously when he approaches and Scott stares back at them defiantly. After his firing from the show, even though he was a teenager at the time, a part of Scott wanted to believe that Miranda would help him but by then the show was less about Miranda and more about the new Axel.

"It's good to have you back Scotty." Axel says with fake sincerity. Scott frowns and nods toward the Bible.

"What are you doing with that?" Scott asks and the life-size Axel looks down at the book in their hands and shrugs.

"A better question is what are *you* doing with it? We already discussed what this kind of propaganda is encouraging in Kieri and yet you haven't thrown it out yet although you've had plenty of opportunity." Axel replies.

"I'll throw it out when I feel like it." Scott replies simply in defiance of the merperson, knowing he did not owe them any explanation. The memory of what happened in Mr. Stoddard's office that day was making Scott bitter and angry all over again.

"Scott there is no reason for you to keep this book around, and Kieri should be punished for having it." Axel replies to Scott before addressing the children. "Isn't that right young ones?" Axel asks the children at their feet in the sand.

"That's right!" The children shout in unison. Scott, who until then had forgotten he and Axel were not alone, looks closely at the children and their appearances horrify him, as the kids look vastly different now. They are all still wearing their boarding school uniforms but their faces have this strange solid look as if they have no muscles to distinguish expressions. Their eyes are larger and glassy looking now, like two empty black orbs on their faces. Their mouths are larger too; the corners of their lips stretching back nearly to their ears so when they talk their jaws drop down then pull up again in rhythm to the speech without the lips forming actual words, like a puppet. Scott steps back slowly from the children and stares at Axel who smiles back at him with a more distinctive facial expression and human looking eyes now.

"What happened to them? What's wrong with their faces?" Scott asks Axel, who merely shrugs.

"What do you mean Scotty? The children look the same way they always have. And don't change the subject; I want you to get rid of this book and punish Kieri for having it." Axel replies in a commanding tone and Scott shrinks back as if he were in Arthur's office all over again.

"If Kieri wants to read it, she has a right to." Scott whispers, while trying to keep an eye on both Axel and the "children".

"If Kieri has a right to read it, why did you take it from her room in the first place? Scotty, you obviously have a problem with the change in her too, so why do we sound like we're disagreeing?" Axel asks with fake concern as if trying not to fight. Scott cannot think of an answer so he tries to change the subject again.

"A better question is why didn't you help me when I told Mr. Stoddard about the abuse, about Teague and what he was doing to me and Grayson? I needed you, actually I needed Miranda but neither of you were there. Grayson wasn't even there and he's the one who talked me into saying something. He thought if I spoke up, that I wouldn't get fired because I was the star of the show, and I was stupid enough to believe him." Scott says and Axel does a strange head motion as a human would do if they were rolling their eyes at someone's childish behavior.

"Scotty, if I could have done anything at all, I would've stopped you from saying anything and losing your job. You have to understand the world you live in has a price for everything. Margo understands that cost or at least she used to and Grayson understood it, which is why he didn't get fired." Axel replies and Scott looks at them sharply.

"He also didn't live past the age of 21, and I think that says a lot more about his decision making." Scott replies with a growing sadness; he was still angry with Grayson but his anger often had to combat with the deep pain inside of him due to the loss of his friend.

"We all have our weaknesses. Your weakness tends to be taking things out of context. However, that is in the past now and we should not focus on it anymore. What I want to know is why you still have this Bible?" Axel asks again and Scott stares at the oversized puppet and the deformed children. Honestly, he did not know why he still had the Bible. He wanted to throw it away the night he found it and every night after, but instead he found himself sitting at the kitchen island late each night with a bowl of cereal and the book open in front of him.

"I don't know why but I just didn't have the energy to throw it out before." Scott explains without looking at Axel directly.

"But you have the energy to read it." Axel replies sharply and Scott is a little startled by their tone.

"I was only flipping through it a little, there's no harm in that." Scott replies.

"Is that so? What if Kieri started out by just flipping through it a little?" Axel asks sarcastically and Scott shrugs.

"I didn't say I believed in any of it, I just said I was flipping through it." Scott replies with unease.

"Then throw it out Scott. Instead of imitating Kieri, you should be focused on how to make her see her mistakes." Axel explains.

"I'll toss it out just before the garbage truck shows up so she won't see it in the trash." Scott replies.

"Make sure that you do!" Axel snaps and Scott looks at them.

"I said that I would! Why are you so worried about a book anyway? You don't even believe in that sort of thing; it has nothing to do with whatever you're doing here." Scott replies and when Axel flips their emerald green tail in the air Scott notices that the scales of their tail are not shiny like before. Actually, the scales are beginning to look a dark mossy color like wet wool.

"It's not about what I believe in, it's about who believes in me and I don't like competition. My issue with this book is what it is doing to your daughter and is now doing to you. I'm here to help you and your family as I always do because I'm your friend. Anytime you had a problem, I was there for you because you had no one else. Then one day you found someone else and you left me. Now that you're back, I know this book and what it teaches is going to take you away from me again." Scott catches the bitterness in Axel's voice as memories of the shows abrupt end come back to him. After the show's cancellation, the fate of Miranda/Axel was never explored or further explained.

"You didn't help me with all of my problems." Scott replies, though his heart is still heavy with guilt at abandoning Miranda.

"I did try to, you just didn't listen. I knew if they fired you that would be the end of us all. Now you're so bitter that you have a chance to right the wrongs that happened to both of us and you're not going to take it. You don't even care about giving me new life do you?" Axel asks with a sad voice.

"I can't do that show again Axel, it's not …" Scott struggles to find the right words, as he had not told anyone specifically why he was so against the reboot, not even AJ; as Scott had been using his cold the past few days to avoid the issue altogether.

"Yes you can Scotty! You got your happily ever after, why can't I have mine?" Axel asks with a strained voice. "No one knew what happened to me and it wasn't fair that I was just forgotten. This could be a new beginning for me and you are my bridge Scotty, to a new world and a more accepting time. While you're all grown up now and raising a family of your own there are other children out there, just like these here, who need my help." Axel looks fondly at the children. "They need to know that someone understands them and that they are not bad or wrong for wanting to be their true selves. There are other *Kailas* out there that need me Scotty, and you can bring me to them and to Kieri. I could be what draws you two back together as a father and daughter, after God drove you two apart. Kieri needs to know that what she believes in is not right and that if she doesn't change she'll suffer much worse this time around than being sent to a foster home." Axel replies calmly and Scott looks alarmed.

"Don't talk about my daughter like that! Don't threaten her! And who told you I have a happily ever after kind of life?" Scott snaps and Axel smiles.

"I'm not threatening her Scotty, but she's a bully and you are happy, aren't you?" Axel replies in more of a command than a question. Scott ignores the issue of his own happiness to focus on Axel's threat toward Kieri.

"Kieri isn't bullying anyone, and if anyone so much as lays a hand on my daughters …" Scott begins but Axel interrupts.

"You'll do what Scotty? You can't fight the whole world, you can't even fight yourself, you're the one who got angry about the things she said and sent her away in the first place remember? I'm just saying that the God Kieri follows is not leading her in the direction the rest of the world is going in and He's setting Kieri up to get hurt. If you want to protect her, you have to teach her about acceptance and maybe about compromise. No one minds if she still believes in Him but at the same time, she has to live by the world's openness and 'go with the flow' as they say. It is safer for her to walk with us and not offend anyone. You do want to keep her safe, don't you?" Axel asks and Scott looks up at the sky. The light from the fully risen sun is blinding him. As the sunlight beams down on him from one direction, he shades his eyes with his arm only to have another sun shining on him from the other side.

"What is this, why is it so bright out?" Scott asks as he raises both arms to protect himself but the light is becoming more intense as there now seems to be more than a dozen "suns" in the sky all shining down on him. Scott looks at Axel and their hair has changed from short white blonde locks into short strands of white blonde yarn.

"Scotty, I need you to pay attention, I need you to listen to me!" Axel commands but Scott looks away at the open sea to find his ship is now not much larger than the toy tugboat Riah plays with in the bathtub.

"What happened to my ship?" Scott asks, as the little boat is not that far out but has actually shrunk down dramatically in size and Scott takes a few steps toward the water in alarm. Now he can see even the water has changed, it is no longer liquid but strange solid wave shapes that seem to be cut out of cardboard or some other hard material and painted blue; rows and rows of cut out beach waves alternatively shifting mechanically left and right across the floor.

"Scotty, I need you to listen to me!" Axel howls and their voice has become raspy and deep. Scott looks back at Axel the Merperson who still looks like a life-size puppet but now seems to be made of both fabric material and human flesh crudely stitched together. Scott stumbles backward, horrified and falls into the fake ocean.

CHAPTER THIRTEEN

Scott rolls out of the bed and lands on the cold hardwood floor. He lies on the ground for a moment in the dark trying to hold on to his dream but it quickly fades. Whatever he had seen from his subconscious mind scared him enough that he rolled right off the edge of the bed. Scott sits up slowly hoping AJ did not hear him fall, before he remembers that he is in another guest bedroom on the first floor. When Scott got sick he moved into a separate room as AJ had a severe case of germophobia and it worked out for the best especially after their argument in the kitchen.

Scott stands up slowly, grabs his phone off the dresser and leaves the room. Scott enters the kitchen to carry out his usual late night custom of eating a bowl of cereal and reading a chapter or two from Kieri's Bible. Scott prepares himself a snack first but as he reaches under the sink for the book, he realizes that it is not there. Scott crosses the kitchen toward the doorway of the sitting room. He is oblivious to the small lamp light on the table between the two large chairs in the sitting room. One chair is occupied, but Scott does not notice as he begins looking through the trashcan for the Bible, fearing someone may have found it and thrown it away.

"What are you looking for?" Scott jumps, startled by AJ's voice, and removes his foot from the trash lid pedal causing the lid to slam back down with an echoing clang. Both men remain frozen, waiting to hear if the noise woke anyone. Once the following silence assures them that everyone is still asleep, AJ laughs slightly.

"Sorry, I didn't even do that on purpose, but I've always wanted to scare someone like that." AJ is sitting in one of the large high-backed chairs by the fireplace, which is unlit. The small lamp on the table beside AJ casts a strange shadow over his face making him look weary and grim.

"I was just looking for … I was just looking to see if anyone had finished off the juice." Scott answers quickly as he raises the empty fruit juice cartoon out of the trash then lets it drop back into the bin.

"There's orange juice in there that might be a little better for your cold." AJ suggests and Scott nods if only to pull away from the awkward encounter. Scott takes the water filter out of the refrigerator instead and fills his glass. Scott stands at the island playing with his bowl of cereal, as he has suddenly lost his appetite, while AJ watches him. From his spot in the kitchen, Scott can see the illustrated Bible in AJ's lap. AJ notices that Scott can see the book and he frowns.

"I wasn't sure how to tell you about this. I found it under the sink and I was going to confront Kieri about it in the morning. I didn't want to tell you because I didn't want you to get angry with her again. I had no idea she was still reading this stuff." AJ explains and Scott exhales while trying to look clueless on the matter.

"I figured she wouldn't give it up too easily." Scott replies and AJ nods.

"I want to apologize to you for not telling you about the apartment and about not being upfront on wanting to move here. Honestly, I didn't know how to tell you. I don't mean to keep secrets when it comes to matters of our parenting or our marriage; it's just that I don't feel I can tell you things because you treat me like a child. You don't allow my input on anything and you don't let us come to some kind of agreement or a middle ground. Especially with the girls, you act as if your word is the final word, and I wish you understood how that makes me feel because I am their father too. At the same time, I realize that there is no excuse for keeping secrets. Margo has been helping us with the rent for the past year now but she can't do it anymore. Our trust fund is drying up and we really don't have anything left except this estate. Which I personally think is beneficial since this house can be a home for all of us. It can be a new beginning and with Kieri getting older, it might help to have a woman around now? You know someone Kieri can talk to that understands girl problems. Someone she can ask the questions that she might be too embarrassed to come to us for." AJ explains and Scott frowns.

"AJ, she's fifteen, whatever she thought she needed to know from a woman I'm sure she's picked up by now from other sources and personally I think the window for motherly guidance is pretty small at this point for both Margo and Kieri." Scott replies and AJ shrugs.

"Well that's just more proof that she never needed a mother in the first place if she made it this far without one. What is really on my mind is that I don't want to lose you or our children, we already lost one." AJ looks in pain and Scott feels empathy for him. Amid the chaos, the anger, and the doubt he really did not want to see AJ hurt and he did not want to lose his girls either. Scott enters the room and sits in the empty chair beside AJ.

"AJ I know that they are *our* kids and that we should parent them equally as a team. It's just that I only had my mother growing up and the way she pushed me into acting really took all the fun out of my childhood, if there ever was any to begin with. To make things worse she never defended me from anything and that's really what I'm trying to do with our daughters, to protect them. I want them to know that I will protect them if anyone tried to hurt them." Scott cannot bring himself to say more than that so he switches directions slightly. "I don't want the girls to be forced to do anything they don't want to do. Shows like *Oliver* put children in danger by exposing them to predators and people who would take advantage of them and I don't want anything happening to Kieri or Riah." Scott says while still wanting to explain more, but he is unable to manage the words.

"You'll be on the show too Scott." AJ says. "You won't be distant like your mother and I'll be there. We can protect them, we always have. If Kieri says no to something the answer is no. Anyone who signs on for this reprisal would know that they need us more than we need them and Margo will be on board if you are; which means most of the production decisions will be in our hands and the girls will be perfectly safe." AJ explains with excitement and Scott immediately doubts this but does not say so aloud.

"I still feel like that's going to be a problem." Scott says as he nods to the Bible in AJ's hands. "I mean I don't want to hinder our daughters in exploring their faith, even if that faith is somewhat difficult to take in, but what's in there doesn't line up with shows like *Oliver's Explorations*." Scott explains while fearing that he may have revealed too much of his growing interest in the Bible. AJ does not seem to notice though.

"I don't want to hinder Kieri either but I wish she understood that not everything is so black and white. I mean it's just a role, playing a character that doesn't fit with the standards of the Bible doesn't mean someone doesn't love God. It just means they like acting and not everyone in the entertainment industry is a heathen or an atheist. Even Margo believes in God and all those voodoo witch roles and demonic granny characters she played before she retired didn't change that." AJ replies.

"It's more than just a role AJ. The character a person plays can sometimes become their life when you immerse yourself in everything, including their emotions and thoughts. What makes them happy or sad makes you happy or sad; what frightens them frightens you, what angers them, angers you, what afflicts them afflicts you; what they love, you love, what they hate, you hate. Oliver the Orphan became Scott the Orphan. I felt abandoned just like him and, well you saw how that turned out. I think for Kieri it's more than her playing a role, it's what that role or that character does to influence a person watching her. Even Margo had her issues with some of the characters she played, why else would she have had that breakdown?" Scott asks and AJ shakes his head.

"Margo had a breakdown because she couldn't cope with getting older, just like her mother. Playing a crazy old witch living in a swamp is a big change up from the hot college coed getting chased by a masked killer." AJ explains.

"I think there was a little more to it than that AJ. Admittedly, even I was a little ashamed of Oliver coming out as gay. I mean I was still coming to terms with my own sexuality by then and I was a teenager; children Riah's age used to watch that show and maybe, it did confuse them a little. And consider what happens in movies, when two characters have a one-night stand that leads to true love; that's not reality, yet someone out there who is so desperate for love will believe that meaningless sex with a stranger is the only way to that and they'll get left with a broken heart, or worse." Scott explains as best he can. AJ may have grown up on the set of a show but he was not an actor and he could never really understand what it meant to lose your identity for a narrative or the manipulation that pours out of a character and an intriguing story line.

"I wish you and Margo would stop acting like it's wrong to teach children about homosexuality. It's better that they learn it young and then they won't struggle to understand themselves as they get older. And this should be easier for Kieri and Riah, they're basically playing themselves and they won't have to do anything they don't normally do." AJ explains as Scott stares at the Bible.

"AJ, I don't want them forced into anything; I don't want anyone trying to convince either of them to say yes to something they might be against or even hesitate about. Even if Riah puts up a fuss, the answer is no for her too." Scott replies calmly and AJ nods.

"I understand that and I agree with you, which is why I want you to talk to Kieri about it." AJ says while recalling his previous conversation with Kieri, back in his father's office. "I already tried to talk to her and I don't think it did much good. I'm sorry I didn't listen to you either, when you told me about her behavior and what she was reading and saying. This book is just about enforcing a bunch of laws and pointless commandments that are long overdue for rewrites. It's not even applicable now in modern day. That aside, you and Kieri were best friends once and I know she still loves you, even after everything that's happened. Maybe if you talk to her, if you convince her that this whole Christianity thing is hurting us, that it's hurting her future, maybe she'll give a little. And I think if you ask her to do the show, she'll do it." AJ explains.

"AJ if she's not listening to you, I doubt she'll listen to me. I'm the father who sent her away remember?" Scott replies, not really wanting to convince Kieri to do the show and AJ rests a consoling hand on his shoulder.

"She's still your little princess, don't worry. Every family has issues like us, let's just hope this is as bad as it gets." AJ replies as he holds the Bible up examining it. "It might be best if I throw this out?" AJ suggests and Scott tries to hide his alarm.

"Well maybe when I talk to Kieri I can give it back to her? I mean not everything in it is so exclusive or divisive and I don't think she'll feel very free to express herself if every time she gets a Bible we're throwing it away. I'll just explain to her that she can keep the Bible with the understanding that she stops trying to preach to everyone and that she realizes that she shouldn't take everything in it literally. If she doesn't agree to that, I'll throw it out myself." Scott offers and AJ hesitates but concedes anyway and hands the book to Scott who takes it while trying to hide his relief.

CHAPTER FOURTEEN

Kieri was still in grade school the first time she ever received a real punishment for anything. Up until that point, she and Kyrie misbehaved like any other children, but when they did so, the punishment was not much more than a scolding or time out in the corner of the room, given to them by one of their fathers while the other tried to make up for it with overcompensating kindness and treats. This time was different though as AJ felt it was necessary to be very firm in punishing Kieri even though he would not explain why she was in trouble or at least Scott did not understand his explanation.

"I don't care what you say, she is not coming out of that room for the rest of the month, other than to eat, use the bathroom and go to school." AJ explained as he cleared the dinner plates from the table. Scott had just returned home that evening from a promotional tour for one of his artists. Instead of excited greetings upon his return, Scott was met with AJ's frustrations over Scott being away for so long and two silent children, one of whom was immediately banished to her room as soon as dinner was over.

"That's nearly the entire month, come on AJ she didn't even do anything." Scott pled Kieri's case.

"That's exactly why she's being punished. *She didn't do anything* and she should've done something or said something." AJ snapped back as he loaded the dishwasher.

"AJ, they are children in grade school, they are not political activists. You're putting too much on them instead of just allowing them to be kids." Scott explained as he considered the changes that had been happening before and during his trip. A few months earlier, their son Kyrie had begun calling himself Kaila and he expected the rest of the house to do the same. AJ explained to Scott before he left that it was best to honor their "daughter's" wishes as Kaila was finally coming out of her shell to embrace her new identity. Scott was still struggling to process the situation when he came home and saw his son … daughter with longer hair and glitter nail polish sitting at the dinner table looking regretful most likely because he … she was the cause of all the trouble.

"I'm not putting too much on them! I am trying to strengthen them and prepare them for the real world which is a harsh place and I'm trying to teach them that I can't defend them forever and eventually they will need to stand up for themselves and each other. It's bad enough I get no help from you, you're hardly even here. Do you know how difficult it is to do this by myself? I'm here alone for weeks at a time trying to keep a nice home for you and do the best I can with our children while trying to balance my own career on top of that and as soon as you get back all I catch from you is flak because you don't like how I'm doing things." AJ argued and Scott tried to diffuse the situation a little too late.

"I wasn't trying to …" Scott began but AJ cut him off.

"Oh, I know exactly what you were trying to do, so you want Kieri off punishment, take her off punishment! Undermine me like you always do, I mean she's more your daughter than she is mine right!" AJ shouted as he slammed the dishwasher shut and stormed out of the room leaving Scott alone in the dining room of their old condominium.

Scott knocked on the twin's bedroom door with a sign that read, "No boys allowed" taped to the center, although they shared the room.

"Come in." Kieri replied from the inside. Scott entered the room to find Kieri alone seated on the edge of her bed reading a book.

"Where's your, um, where's your sister?" Scott asked and Kieri shrugged, visibly annoyed.

"I don't know, probably in the TV room, it's where I'd be." Kieri replied and Scott shut the door behind him and sat on Kyrie/Kaila's bed.

"So I heard you got into some trouble this week, you want to tell me what happened?" Scott asked and Kieri shrugged again.

"There's nothing to tell. I called Kaila, Kyrie and I got in trouble." Kieri explained simply while she tried to pretend she was still reading her book.

"There's a lot more to it than that I'm sure." Scott replied.

"Well I'm already on punishment for it so why does it matter?" Kieri asked and Scott nodded.

"That's true, you are on punishment now. I'm just hoping to get you off punishment by getting your side of the story." Scott replied.

"I don't have a side Dad." Kieri replied and Scott looked around the room for something he could use to help him in this situation. Last month Kieri had a slumber party to celebrate the end of summer. She invited all of her friends over and out of the six that did come, two went home early when they realized that Kieri's twin, whom they still saw as a boy, would be joining the all-girl party with them. On her desk was a notebook labeled truth or dare that Scott heard the kids playing that night. Scott picked the notebook up but Kieri noticed and was quick to retrieve the book from his hands.

"That's private." Kieri exclaimed as she took the notebook and shoved it under her pillow.

"Sorry, I didn't know kids still played that game. How about I challenge you to a round of truth or dare?" Scott asked and Kieri looked uncertain until he raised his arms to show he had nothing up his sleeve, physically or metaphorically. "It's just a game and you got nothing to lose, unless you're hiding some secrets from me but then again you'll learn my secrets too." Scott explained. This seemed to put Kieri at ease so she sat up and set the book down.

"Okay, but I get to ask first; truth or dare?" Kieri asked and Scott pretended to think.

"Dare." Scott replied. Kieri dared her father to balance on one leg for sixty seconds and Scott stumbled around the room highly exaggerating his terrible balance, just to get his daughter to laugh. It worked and she chose dare next as well so he dared her to do a backflip, which Scott already knew she could do to perfection. They went back and forth for a few minutes daring each other to do silly physically maneuvers until it was Kieri's turn to ask again and this time Scott picked truth. Kieri paused and stared at her father for a moment.

"Is this game secret? I mean we're not allowed to tell anyone else what we said?" Kieri asked and Scott nodded.

"Absolutely secret; nothing admitted here leaves this room. Now ask me anything." Scott assures her.

"Do you really love Papa AJ? I mean like, love-love, like how my friend's dads love their moms?" Kieri asked with sincerity and somewhat confusion to her fathers' relationship as theirs was like no other marriage she had seen among her friends. Scott was caught off guard by the question. No one had ever asked him that in such a way as to inspire a genuine response, not even the minister that married him and AJ. Scott forced a smile before he answered.

"Of course I love your father; I love him so much I married him." Scott replied and Kieri frowned, perhaps because she expected a different answer or because she did not fully believe he was telling the truth and to be honest, that night, he felt a little guilty at the idea that maybe he was not.

"Okay, your turn, I choose truth." Kieri replied and Scott pushed down his feelings of conviction.

"Okay, did you know Kaila's teacher was calling her Kyrie?" Scott asked and Kieri nodded. Scott wanted to believe that it was a mistake on AJ's part and that Kieri did not know what the teacher was doing or why it was wrong as Kieri was not even in her teens yet so Scott did not expect her to see everything as something to be offended by. The twins had just started school a week earlier and while there was no legal change; it was over the summer that Kyrie had switched to Kaila. AJ either did not have enough time or just forgot to enroll him under a new name and his chosen gender as female prior to school beginning. The first day AJ informed the school that Kyrie wished to be addressed as Kaila and identified as a girl. AJ also wanted her teacher informed of the change so she could address Kaila accordingly; the teacher did not address Kaila accordingly.

"Were you still calling her Kyrie too?" Scott asked and Kieri frowned.

"It's my turn dad; truth or dare?" Kieri replied in objection and Scott looked apologetic.

"Sorry, I pick truth." Scott replied and Kieri chewed her bottom lip while thinking.

"Did you always like boys?" Kieri asked and Scott was unprepared for her question yet again.

"Depends on what you mean by *always*? I mean there was a time in my life when I didn't like anyone, just like any other kid. Okay yes, I guess if you mean when I first started feeling attracted to people, my first crush was a boy." Scott replied, recalling how he was coached to respond to that very same question back in his youth whenever he did interviews for *Oliver's Explorations*. "Even my first kiss was with a boy." Scott added while omitting how that experience had been under some coaching as well but Kieri accepted his answer anyway.

"Okay, truth, I always called Kyrie by his name. When we started school, the teacher called him Kyrie too and she told Dad she heard me say it whenever I would pick him up after class. I don't like him to be outside too long by himself because the other kids try to beat him up. Dad got mad at me for confusing Kyrie's teachers and said I was in trouble for using his dead name." Kieri explained more than she needed to, for a reason and Scott could not look at her directly as he sympathized with her frustrations on the issue but did not want to admit it or correct her for using the wrong pronouns either.

Along with his anger at Kieri, AJ vented to Scott that the admin at the school did not see it as a big deal to call Kyrie by his birth name or to address him as male, as they were simply following what was on his birth certificate. When AJ tried to dispute this accusing the school of transphobia and discrimination, the principal was quick to point out that if AJ saw his son as a daughter now he would have made the necessary changes before school began.

"Kieri, you know that was wrong, Kaila is her name now and you *are* confusing people by calling her Kyrie." Scott explained as Kieri picked at a thread on her blanket.

"That's not how the game works dad." Kieri replied, sulking.

"We're not playing the game anymore." Scott replied. "This is real life and your twin is going through a real struggle. Your Papa AJ wants to ground you for a month, which I think is a little excessive, but I need you to help me help you. Kaila needs the support of her whole family right now; actually, she needs your support more than anyone else because you are her sister and this is just you being stubborn. Her name is Kaila now." Scott repeated emphatically and Kieri looked at him in anger.

"Why is it Kaila now? All my life I had a brother not a sister and now, over the summer he just changed and everyone expects me to pretend that I didn't have a brother a year ago. My brother's not dead and I don't like Kaila!" Kieri's voice cracked as she began to cry and Scott stood up to comfort her but she shrank back from him. He did not expect that kind of reaction and he was ashamed that Kieri was bold enough to say aloud what he was thinking and feeling on the inside. Scott knew he had to be accepting of this change for Kaila's mental health, but it was hard and now he was realizing just how difficult it was for Kieri. He walked to the door, defeated and prepared to leave but Kieri stopped him.

"It's still my turn dad." Kieri demanded.

"I told you we're not playing the game anymore Kieri, but I think a week of punishment is enough, instead of a month, enough time for you to think about what's best for Kaila." Scott replied while he tried to sound authoritative but felt ridiculous.

"I don't care about my punishment; I want to finish the game." Kieri replied and Scott gave her a sharp look.

"You're really pushing it young lady." Scott replied but after a moment, he conceded. "Truth and after this the game is over." Scott said. Kieri sat up and stared at him.

"Does it bother you that Dad loves other men when you're not home?" Kieri asked and Scott felt a punch in his gut. AJ said all that was over. Scott could not come up with a lie fast enough to answer such a question with dignity.

"You win." Scott mumbled and left the room to go sleep on the couch.

CHAPTER FIFTEEN

The next morning, Scott and Kieri return to the manor with a car full of groceries from town. The two ride in awkward silence together as Scott replays their game of truth or dare in his mind. Although it was so long ago, he is still in awe over Kieri's willingness to speak up about things that bother her while Scott feared reprisal and eventually learned to keep quiet a long time ago. After Kieri's punishment, AJ tried to sue the school claiming harassment, discrimination and mental distress for Kaila as the school refused to accommodate any changes for her chosen name and gender. That was until AJ had all the formal paperwork changed on Kaila's behalf, so nothing reached a courtroom and the whole matter was settled privately. Almost immediately, the school became *overly* accommodating to the point of celebrating Kaila's transitioning. Allowing Kaila to take physical education with the other girls, even though this caused problems with the parents who did not want their daughter's sharing a locker room with a biological boy. Some families opted to remove their children from the school entirely. Kaila's teacher soon quit after the school directors tried to force her into some kind of transgender appreciation course to instruct her on how to inquire of her student's pronouns and chosen names, as if the poor woman did not have enough work on her hands, and last Scott heard she moved out of state.

"Do you remember that game of truth or dare that we played when you were a kid?" Scott asks. He told AJ the previous night that he would talk to Kieri about the show and about her faith, and he planned to keep his word, though not in the way he may have led AJ to believe. Out of the many things he wanted to talk to his daughter about, convincing her to do that ridiculous show was not on his list. Kieri looks at her father while trying to remember.

"You mean when you grounded me?" Kieri replies with a playful smirk.

"Your Papa AJ grounded you; I believe I was the one trying to get you off of punishment." Scott recalls and Kieri nods.

"I'm sorry for what I said to you about Papa AJ." Kieri replies after a moment, remembering how she wanted to rub it in her father's face that his husband was unfaithful to him. Her Papa AJ's infidelities were just another part of their family life that never felt right to Kieri, no matter how her Papa AJ tried to justify it or normalize it.

"You had a right to say it, you were angry." Scott replies as if it did not bother him though years later the comment still stings. He never confronted AJ about it, among other things.

"I didn't have any right to disrespect you. The Bible says not to do that, and for children to respect their parents and listen to them."[11] Kieri explains.

"Listen to them too?" Scott asks and Kieri shrugs.

"Well, maybe listen to them when they're telling you to follow God." Kieri adds and Scott nods.

"I figured there was a catch somewhere. Do you really agree with everything you read in the Bible? I mean, do you *follow* everything you read in the Bible?" Scott asks and Kieri shrugs again.

"I haven't read it all yet, but I try to follow what I understand." Kieri explains.

"Why do you believe it?" Scott asks and Kieri shifts uncomfortably.

---

[11] EXODUS 20:12/PROVERBS 6:20 (NKJV)

"I just do." Kieri replies simply and Scott glances at her briefly as he turns into the manor driveway.

"I know there's more to it than that." Scott replies and Kieri remains silent. "Well it's my turn, so truth or dare." Scott asks.

"That's not going to work this time, you said I won before." Kieri replies and looks down at her phone.

"Well I lied, you didn't win and now it's my turn, so truth or dare?" Scott asks again.

"Technically I did win because you didn't answer my last question." Kieri explains.

"You just apologized for asking it." Scott counters.

"I apologized for bringing it up because I did it to be cruel at the time, but I did still ask and you didn't answer, which means I won and the game is over." Kieri explains and Scott thinks for a moment.

"It does bother me, it bothered me back then and it still hurts now. I hope that if you get married someday, that your husband never betrays you like that and if he does, I hope you are stronger than I am and that you don't put up with it. You're better off single than wasting your love on someone who takes it for granted." Scott answers honestly for the first time to Kieri's surprise as she can sense he is telling her the truth.

"Now I feel even worse for asking. Okay I pick dare." Kieri replies softly and Scott smiles to ease her conscience.

"I dare you to carry all the groceries inside in one trip by yourself." Scott says and Kieri jumps out of the passenger seat and begins loading all the bags onto her arms and waddling comically into the house.

Kieri sets the bags on the counter in triumph and Scott begins to unload the bags.

"Good job, I choose dare too." Scott replies and Kieri helps him unload the bags as she is thinking of something to dare him to do. As she is putting some boxes into the cabinet, Kieri looks out the window, past the garden and into the dark woods.

"I dare you to climb one of those trees in the woods." Kieri replies and Scott looks at her incredulously.

"Are you kidding me, I didn't even climb trees when I was your age." Scott replies as he puts the last of the perishable food away and leads Kieri outside.

They enter the woods and Scott searches for a decent tree with enough branches he can get a grip on. He finds one but after getting a grip on the first branch, he cannot reach the next so he drops back down and looks at Kieri.

"You can always admit defeat dad, there's no shame in it." Kieri suggests with a smile.

"Not this time." Scott replies with renewed strength as he spots a new tree and begins to climb up. He manages to get his feet off the ground and he is a full foot high in the air pulling his body up higher when his support branch breaks and he falls back down landing on his back. Kieri shouts in alarm and runs to her father who is laughing while lying on his back in the dirt.

"I'm okay and you never said how high I had to climb so consider that dare accomplished." Scott replies as he sits up slowly.

"Dad seriously, you could've broken your neck." Kieri replies as she helps Scott to his feet and he begins to brush the dirt and leaves off the back of his pants.

"Well you're the one who dared me to do it." Scott counters.

"Yeah because I thought it would be easy for you, how was I supposed to know you've never climbed a tree before?" Kieri asks and Scott laughs at her.

"Okay, my turn, truth or dare?" Scott asks as he leans against the tree for a minute to catch his breath.

"I pick truth, just so nobody else gets hurt playing this stupid game." Kieri replies.

"Okay, do you really believe your father and I are going to hell?" Scott asks in a serious tone and Kieri hesitates for a moment.

"I don't know Dad." Kieri replies, not wanting to hurt or offend her father again.

"No really, no hurt feelings in this game, I just want your honest opinion, your truth." Scott explains and Kieri exhales deeply and stares down the path deeper into the woods.

"I do, the Bible says it's wrong and specifically that people who live like you and Dad won't inherit the kingdom of heaven, which means they won't go to heaven, I think.[12] And when a person dies, there's only one of two places they can go." Kieri answers and Scott nods while trying to hide how much this truth bothers him.

"Okay, my turn." Kieri says and Scott stands up straight.

"Dare." Scott replies only to irritate her and Kieri frowns at first until an idea comes to mind.

"Okay, I dare you to show me that statue in the woods." Kieri replies and now Scott frowns.

"Of course somebody told you about that stupid statue. Kieri I don't want to go all the way out there." Scott replies and Kieri shakes her head.

---

[12] 1 CORINTHIANS 6:9-10 (NKJV)

"You picked dare Dad, do it or lose the game." Kieri reminds him and Scott motions for her to follow him as by now he can remember his way back to where he found Margo the day she fell.

"Alright, well let's keep the game going on the walk. Are you picking truth again?" Scott asks and Kieri nods but says nothing. "Okay, where else in the Bible does it say that homosexuality is wrong?" Scott asks and Kieri tries to think.

"Well that's not a truth type of question for this game but I'll take it." Kieri replies. "From what I remember, there are a couple of different chapters, there wasn't a lot on the subject in the children's Bible but in the adult version I read, there were two chapters that stood out to me. The first was Genesis chapter 2; it's indirect on the subject until you dig a little deeper around the part when God made Eve to be a companion for Adam. After God made Adam, God said it wasn't good for man to be alone and that God would make a helper comparable to Adam. So God made animals and Adam named them all but the Bible said there wasn't any animal comparable to Adam so God put Adam to sleep and took Adam's rib and with the rib He made a woman who was later named Eve. A friend of mine, when I was away, she said that she believed that what God took from Adam to make a woman, represented an important part that men are missing that women have and what women are missing men have and together under God they make a complete one." Kieri explains without divulging her friend's identity, but Scott can imagine Kieri and the unknown Mrs. B. having this conversation, even though he has never met the woman before.

"My friend also said a man coming together with another man in that way can't make up for what they are missing because they are both men lacking the same thing; just as two women together wouldn't work because they are also lacking the same thing so they can't truly become one. What my friend said reminded me of you and Dad and how you two seem really incompatible." Kieri replies cautiously but Scott is listening intently and does not seem angry, just curious, so she quickly addresses the second verse. "A more direct verse though, is in Romans 1, God said that women with other women is going against nature and men leaving the natural relationship they could have with women so they could be with men was also against nature and sinful and that there is a punishment for it internally and externally." As Kieri speaks, Scott remembers his last conversation with Grayson. "Anyway, the way it's described in the Bible is that gay relationships are unnatural and unhealthy, physically, spiritually and mentally too." Kieri explains and Scott can feel the frustration growing inside of him.

"If that were the case and it was so unnatural, why does God draw men to other men and women to other women?" Scott asks and Kieri can sense the anger in his voice as they continue walking but she does not let it deter her this time.

"It's not your turn Dad, but I will say this, it's not always God who draws people together but when He does it's on a different level than just physical." Kieri replies and Scott sags in defeat, her reply reminding him that he started all this.

"Okay, I pick truth." Scott replies as they draw nearer to the clearing where the statue rests.

"Why didn't you throw my Bible away when you had the chance?" Kieri asks and Scott stops to look at her. That morning after he had gotten the Bible back from AJ, Scott returned it to Kieri's room quickly, before he had the chance to change his own mind. In Kieri's room Scott found

Lydia's Bible that Kieri had taken from the office and he held on to that one instead.

"How'd you even know for sure I was the one who took it?" Scott asks and Kieri smiles.

"I didn't know for sure until now and I didn't want to waste a turn finding out. Now that I think about it, it couldn't have been anyone else but you." Kieri replies and Scott frowns.

"Okay, so I took it because I didn't want you reading it anymore. I didn't throw it away because … well actually I was going to throw it away but something stopped me. I thought at first that you might see it in the trash and take it back out so I figured to hide it until I could throw it out later and then, I started reading it." Scott adds. Kieri stops walking this time to look at him.

"What did you read?" She asks with a look of disbelief and Scott shakes his head.

"Not your turn." Scott replies playfully as he leads Kieri into the clearing where they approach the large statue still hidden under the tarp. Scott stops a few feet away and Kieri approaches the statue and clutches the tarp in her fist. She pauses and looks back at Scott.

"What's the tarp for?" Kieri asks and Scott shrugs.

"Probably to protect it from the weather, but if that were the case it was pretty crazy to put it out here in the first place. Your grandfather did that though and he wasn't exactly in the right frame of mind at the time." Scott explains. Kieri pulls the tarp off to reveal the large, distorted image of Axel the Merperson sitting on a rock with a guitar in their hands. Scott frowns, suddenly recalling parts of his dream and the things Axel said to him about Kieri.

"Who is that? Were they giving Miranda a makeover or something?" Kieri asks as she examines the statue with a look of distaste.

"That is Axel the Merperson; they were supposed to be the new mascot of *Oliver's Explorations*; and Miranda's replacement in the season that never got made."

"They? Are you telling me this is supposed to be a *non-binary mermaid*, are you serious? Why would they need this on a children's show?" Kieri asks as she pulls a face.

"I couldn't tell you, but I'll take a guess it was the same reason they had me kissing a boy. I'm just glad they never got a chance to bring them to life." Scott replies as he helps Kieri cover the statue again.

"For some reason I thought the statue would be a little more interesting; probably because Papa AJ seems to care about it so much, but this is just weird. And this is the kind of stuff Dad wants kids to see?" Kieri asks and Scott nods. "Dad, I don't want to do that reboot show, not if this is what it's all about. I hope you're not mad at me, I know Papa AJ will be though." Kieri tries to explain.

"I'm not mad at you, I'm glad you told me how you feel; to be honest I don't want to do the show either. Don't worry about AJ, I'll tell him I won't *let* you do it, then he'll get mad at me, I can deal with that." Scott suggests with a smile and Kieri's face brightens.

"Thanks Dad; okay I pick truth." Kieri says as Scott leads her back out of the clearing.

"When we got into that argument after you got baptized, you said you were afraid that Kaila was in hell, what makes you think that something Kaila did was a sin?" Scott asks and Kieri bites her lip.

"There was this chapter in the Bible in Deuteronomy and it says that it's wrong to wear clothes meant for the opposite gender[13] and I think it means if you're trying to pretend you're the opposite gender than what you are by wearing anything in style of whatever gender you're pretending to be." Kieri explains.

"You mean like a woman wearing pants?" Scott asks.

"No, I mean now it's in fashion for women to wear pants so there are pants made specifically for women and women wear them knowing that they are women. I'm talking about a woman wearing pants that are made for a man and wearing them to look like a man so she can live as a man is wrong. And a man wearing something made for a woman and wearing it so he can look like a woman is wrong too, at least I think that's what the scripture means." Kieri explains as she struggles to phrase her thoughts properly.

"What's so wrong about wearing clothes to pretend to be another gender? Different performers do it all the time and no one is bothered by it." Scott adds, though he can recall a specific time when he was upset with AJ after learning it was a routine of AJ's to take the children to drag shows while Scott was out of town. AJ confessed that he stopped doing this when the shows became a little too graphic in his opinion; though Scott knew the shows had never been suitable for children in the first place. Since AJ cut these trips off when the kids were around seven or eight, Scott decided not to make a big deal of it, believing at the time that they were too young to be affected by it in a negative way and that decision would come back to haunt him after Kaila's death.

---

[13] DEUTERONOMY 22:5 (NKJV)

"Maybe not too many people say out loud that they are bothered by it, by men and women in drag I mean. Some sitcoms and movies put men, especially black men in dresses to emasculate them on purpose, while claiming it's for comedy. As far as the scripture goes, I'm only telling you what I read and how I understood it. Kyrie was wearing girl's clothes, mostly mine, so he could pretend to be something else and reject who God made him to be. I think its offensive to God to try to be something other than what He made you to be. Like in Genesis, the very first chapter; when God created the earth and everything around it and in it, I remember reading it and thinking about Kyrie. Every time God spoke something into existence, the sky, the ocean, the earth, He looked back on what He made and He saw that it was good. He didn't leave anything unfinished or imperfect to His will. What He made was just right for what He intended." Kieri explains as Scott struggles to follow along while thinking about his son.

"And when God made mankind," Kieri continues. "Human beings I mean, He said, 'Let Us make man in Our image, according to Our likeness.'[14] At first that didn't make sense to me, because God was talking about Himself as if He was more than one being. Then my group leader in the Bible study at school explained about the Holy Trinity, God the Father, Jesus Christ the Son, who is also the Word of God and the Holy Spirit of God, He's a guide to everyone who believes. My group leader explained how they were all together when God created everything, including people. My brother believed he was unfinished and I couldn't understand why God would leave him like that in the wrong body." Kieri

---

[14] GENESIS 1:26 (NKJV)

looks near to tears as Scott grabs her hand, squeezing it softly so she will continue.

"So you believed God made him wrong?" Scott asks and Kieri nods.

"I did, until I read Genesis chapter 3, about the serpent, the devil making Eve question things about herself and what God spoke. The serpent convinced Eve that she could be like God if she defied God and ate from the tree. I don't think Eve realized that she was already made in God's image and given authority by God which should've been more than enough. The body God put each of us in is the right body for whatever He has planned for us, but the serpent, the devil comes in to tempt us to chase after more than what we need and to crave things we don't even want. What if the devil and the world tell us we're incomplete, so that we try to compete with God, and try to do things our own way and just mess everything up? The devil rules a corrupted world and he teaches us through the influence in that world to rebel against God and everything good and we call it freedom because we don't realize that rebellion makes us slaves to sin?" Kieri explains and Scott cannot think of anything to say at first. They continue walking in silence with only the sound of the dead leaves crunching under their steps until Scott speaks.

"So you weren't angry at God for taking your twin?" Scott asks and Kieri shrugs.

"Maybe at first, before I really knew Him, God I mean. Eventually I realized that if I could believe that God exists, then there was no reason I couldn't believe the devil exists too. Jesus did say that the thief, the devil, only comes to steal, kill and destroy and Jesus came to give us life.[15] Eventually, I stopped thinking that *if* there was a God, He ruined my

---

[15] JOHN 10:10 (NKJV)

family and I started believing that there *is* a God and He wants to save my family, what's left of it, from the devil who came to destroy us." Kieri explains and Scott is stunned, memories of his own childhood begin running through his mind all at once of a devil tempting him with what he thought he needed and convincing him to crave what he did not really want. All those late nights when Scott was reading from the Bible he had taken from Kieri, he struggled to understand because he was too angry with God to see what was right in front of his face; a truth that his daughter caught on to *because* of her anger, not in spite of it.

"And you really believe that all those stories in the Bible, like about creation of the world and people, actually happened?" Scott asks again cautiously.

"Hey you already tricked me with those extra questions," Kieri replies playfully. "But yes I do believe it all. It's like the more I read it, the more it makes sense." Kieri replies.

"I'm sorry we never sat down and talked about this. I'm sorry that I sent you away. I was doing what I thought was best for you and I know that sounds like the opposite of what happened but, I made a mistake, a lot of mistakes actually." Scott replies and Kieri shrugs.

"I'm sorry for what I said about having you as a dad. I shouldn't have said I was embarrassed about my family, but I am scared for us." Kieri replies and Scott hugs her.

"Okay, take one more turn and I really concede this time and you win." Scott replies as they continue walking and approach the cobblestone path leading back to the garden.

"Okay, truth or dare?" Kieri asks.

"Truth." Scott replies as he can see the entrance of the garden up ahead.

"What part of the Bible did you read?" Kieri asks and Scott tries to remember the story.

"Well I read a few different chapters but there was one you had a bookmark on about these three men that some king was going to burn alive."[16] Scott begins.

"Shadrach, Meshach and Abed-nego!" Kieri adds excitedly and Scott nods.

"Yeah, them, whoever you said. Anyway, the first time I read it I couldn't finish it because I thought the king was the Christian and that he was trying to force the three men to worship a statue of God. Then I went back and I realized that the king was just some person that was trying to make the men who believed in God, bow to a random statue *instead* of God. I was thinking any sane person would just bow to the statue, pretend to worship it and get it over with but then I read another chapter, seemingly at random, about something called the ark of God that these people stole and left in an altar room for their own god. In the room was this statue of the other god, I guess you would call it an idol? The statue of the false god got knocked over when they left the ark of God in the room and the people who worshipped the idol put it back in its place and the next day the statue of the idol was knocked over again and broken and everyone got scared of the ark of God.[17] When I thought about it, I realized that if that false god were real, how did he get knocked over, and why couldn't he put himself back in his place? If he were real, he wouldn't have been broken. Idols in the Bible sound like puppets you have to manipulate or move around to use them and then they're only

---

[16] DANIEL 3 (NKJV)
[17] 1 SAMUEL 5 (NKJV)

good for manipulating people who don't see the hidden figures really pulling the strings. I don't think I could stand against the threat of death like those three men but I can understand now why they refused to submit themselves to that idol." Scott replies while thinking of his dreams of Axel moving on their own. Kieri is about to ask him to explain further but AJ appears in the garden and interrupts them.

"What are you two doing out here? I didn't even realize you were back from the store." AJ says as Scott and Kieri exit the woods looking embarrassed. Scott breaks the awkwardness by kissing Kieri on the top of her head.

"Good game Kiwi." Scott says to Kieri, using her nickname from Riah, before he addresses AJ. "Kieri and I were playing truth or dare, and she won." Scott explains as he heads back into the house, followed by a hopeful looking AJ and a confused Kieri.

CHAPTER SIXTEEN

“What do you mean *you* don’t want to do it? Are you saying this because Kieri said no? Scott I thought you said you would talk to her!” AJ shouts as he paces their guest room while Scott is searching on his phone for flights back home. Scott figured it was best to wait until that evening to tell AJ about his decision though the time of day did not do much for his mood.

“I don’t need to talk to her AJ, I’m saying she doesn’t want to do it and neither do I.” Scott explains as he scrolls through flight destinations searching for the earliest flight on the cheapest airline.

“Okay something isn’t adding up here. You were all for it the other night, so what changed?” AJ asks.

“I was never all for it AJ and it doesn’t matter what changed, my answer is no for me and for Kieri and even if she said yes you still couldn’t do the reboot without me; and I don’t see any reason to reprise such a stupid show in the first place. And correct me if I’m wrong but I’m pretty sure we both agreed if Kieri wasn’t interested that would be the end of it.” Scott adds and AJ frowns.

“Kieri didn’t say she wasn’t interested, *you* said she wasn’t interested, and it’s messing everything up now. I had a theme of the whole family being a part of this.” AJ replies. Scott, realizing what AJ is saying, looks up from his phone and stares at AJ.

“Wait, what do you mean by a theme with the whole family?” Scott asks.

"Just what I said, the whole family meaning you, me, Kieri and Riah. It would've been cute to have a real family playing a television family." AJ replies in a casual manner.

"You never said anything about being on the show, so I take it you were going to play my husband?" Scott asks as more of the story is coming together. Scott always knew AJ wanted to be on *Oliver's Explorations*, but Scott underestimated just how desperate AJ was to be in front of the camera again. AJ looks uncomfortable as he realizes he has revealed too much, too soon.

"Well you might as well know now, that was the idea. Is that such a problem for you, to have me as a husband?" AJ asks as he turns away to stare at his own reflection. Scott shrugs, preparing to let the matter drop until something else occurs to him.

"Wait, I thought you said this script was going to follow the storyline your father started?" Scott asks and AJ nods.

"It is; Oliver and Cody are married now. I mean how else would we fill the role? It's not like Grayson can …" AJ stops talking when he realizes he has offended Scott by being so callous about the death of his friend. "I'm sorry I didn't mean it like that." AJ adds quickly as Scott stands up from the bed and stares at AJ.

"You know what, this is my fault. This whole thing is my fault because I didn't see what was right in front of my face before it got this far. This was never really about Kieri's career, inclusivity, or even saving this estate, this whole thing is about you being in the spotlight and getting the one thing your father would never give you. It was a children's show AJ, a stupid one at that, grow up already and let it go!" Scott shouts and AJ gets defensive.

"I don't even know what you're talking about; I'm not doing this for me. You really think I would hold on to something so stupid like not being on Oliver! And I have grown up, I'm a star in my own right, far from my father's shadow, so don't insult me like that." AJ counters.

"Oh trust me your fame was at the expense of everyone but *you* and don't talk to me like I'm blind. You want to bring Oliver back so you can rub it in your dead father's face for underestimating you. Now I'm glad I'm saying no and I feel even better about saying no for Kieri. If Cody is so easy to recast than so is Oliver and any messed up family they might've had together, so you don't need any of us to kick this reboot off, as a matter of fact, why don't you get the kid who was going to replace me in the final season that never was, to do it? What was his name, Martin something? Last I heard he was running a car dealership and living his best life far from the spotlight, which makes him pretty smart if you ask me." Scott says.

"I never said that Cody was easy to replace and everyone knows you as Oliver so don't act like that! It just made sense that I should take on the role. Besides, who are you to judge me for being angry with my father? You blame your mother for everything that has ever gone wrong in your life and she's been dead for years and you're telling me to grow up!" AJ challenges back. "And since we're getting honest about things why don't we discuss what this is really about? I think it's about time you admitted the real reason you won't let Kieri do this reboot. You're jealous of her just starting out around the same age your career ended. Kieri and I are not responsible for my father's decisions and you had no right to let your bitterness talk our daughter out of taking an opportunity that could be the best thing for her!" AJ argues and Scott takes a few steps back as the accusation takes him by surprise.

"You think this is about jealousy? And that I talked Kieri out of something *good*?" Scott asks and AJ nods.

"She has a chance to be something big. She is beautiful and talented," AJ begins but Scott interrupts him.

"And young and easy to take advantage of. She's the perfect prey for the average predator." Scott replies and AJ rolls his eyes.

"Don't start that again, it's getting so old. Allan Teague was not a child molester and you almost got him fired just because you were mad about being recast on the show." AJ counters. "Allan was a trailblazer who didn't get the respect or credit he deserved for trying to bring gay and trans representation to film and television; and it's not right that he succumbed to the same disease that makes every other gay man a statistic. At least he championed for some kind of change before he died, what have you ever done for our community?" AJ asks and Scott begins to laugh.

"He championed for change, huh? He hosted a few fundraisers, pledging the money to research, which he then stole to prolong his own life. And it's funny you bring up the statistics of gay men, considering how much Teague contributed to the spread of that statistic." Scott replies with all hostility and AJ becomes indignant.

"It was never proven that Grayson contracted anything from Allan and both of them are dead now so I guess we'll never know the truth." AJ replies smugly.

"Oh I know the truth and so do you but you're in denial just like your father and that's not the only thing you two had in common." Scott replies.

"First of all, stop comparing me to him and second of all, I am so sick and tired of people accusing every gay man of being a groomer or a predator or a rapist. Our own children are safer with us as parents than anyone else they could've ended up with." AJ begins but Scott furiously interjects.

"You got some nerve saying that our kids are safe with us!" Scott replies, startling AJ with his tone. "And this has nothing to do with the fact that Teague was gay! He *was* a child molester and he *was* a groomer! I don't know how else to get you to understand that he was a monster and a pedophile and every other horrible thing you can think of. I was a child, left alone with that …that man. He made me do things that I did not want to do, he made me say things I did not want to say, things I didn't believe in. You just don't get it and your father didn't care because you both lived in a protective bubble where nothing bad ever happens or you learn to ignore it so the money doesn't stop flowing. Your father didn't care about what happened to me, Grayson, or any other child. He didn't even care about you or Margo! He let his own daughter run around on film naked, to exploit herself because he never bothered to teach her to have self-value with her clothes on! And you get mad about being compared to him when you exploit our daughters for views on your stupid channel." Scott explains.

"I don't sell my daughters and I have never put them in harm's way." AJ snaps back, but the previous strength in his argument is beginning to wane.

"AJ, you don't know everyone that watches your channel, and there's a reason you get more views on your videos of Riah in the bathtub and in the pool than anything else." Scott replies and AJ looks confused.

"What is this some kind of body issue? She's a toddler, what does she have to show anyone while wearing a bathing suit?" AJ asks completely oblivious.

"You can't be that clueless to the depravity of people. Not everyone is wholesome, not everyone has a pure heart and not all your fans watch your videos with a clean mind or intentions. You had to have some idea of the type of people that might have been watching. The same reason my mother used to shower me with gifts and trips whenever I came back from rehearsals with Allan, she knew what he was doing and she felt guilty, but she didn't feel guilty enough to make it stop. She wanted to think that healing can be bought and it can't." Scott replies as he begins to cry at the memory of the first time and the shame that he carried home. After his firing from the show, Scott told his mother why and she did not seem surprised at all of what Scott accused Teague of, but she got angry that Scott had ruined everything for them. AJ stares at Scott and realizes that he is not acting.

"I don't control the kind of people my fans are but our daughters have never been in danger. You know I would never intentionally film our girls to satisfy some perverts. And if something had happened to you when you were a kid I'm sure there was an explanation." AJ adds. Scott becomes furious.

"*If* something … did you really just say *'if'* for what I just told you?" Scott asks in frustration and AJ sighs.

"I'm not saying you're lying. I'm just saying that memories are not always reliable." Scott begins to walk toward the bathroom and AJ follows him as he speaks. "And a repressed memory suddenly coming to the surface is even worse because it can change with suggestion. Like the lady in the movie that was abused by her mother and had all those personalities and it was supposed to be this huge true story, then this book comes out that the whole thing was made up by her doctor and a writer.

What if what you remember as abuse was just his way of affection?" AJ asks and Scott stands in the doorway of the bathroom staring at AJ.

"I don't have any repressed memories AJ. This one was always with me, always at the front of my mind. I never forgot it, but instead I held onto it, all this time in our marriage, keeping it inside for no real purpose other than the fact that I knew it wouldn't change anything for you. It wouldn't help you see anything differently. And I think in part, I didn't tell you because I thought it would make me weaker, but holding it in kept me weak and now I feel strong." Scott replies softly. "So it doesn't even matter if you believe me or not, what matters is that I don't want Kieri or Riah on that show or any other show like it if there is even the slightest chance someone will do to them what Teague did to me. And you're not filming Riah anymore either." Scott says.

"You don't tell me whether or not I can film my children and I told you they would be perfectly safe." AJ attempts to convince Scott but Scott is not having it.

"You can't promise that! Especially not now, I mean you don't even believe me. What happens if Kieri … if she ever tried to tell you that someone was hurting her, you'd just brush her off too." Scott replies.

"I would not do that to my daughter and I didn't say that I didn't believe you so don't try to guilt me like that. You know that if you told me anything else at any other time I would believe you without question. It just seems a little convenient that you would bring up something like this about a show you were on decades ago, just to convince me that this isn't about jealousy." AJ explains and Scott turns from him and begins to wash his hands.

"You haven't heard a single thing I've said to you. Someone hurt me for years and it changed my life for the worst." Scott explains.

"That someone is long dead. I'm willing to believe that this happened to you but you have to realize that Allan is gone and he's not coming back and Kieri is not in any danger!" AJ counters. Scott shuts the faucet off and faces AJ as he dries his hands.

"Don't patronize me! You think he is the only one in the world that would abuse a child. You think your father is the only one who looked the other way, distracted by money, while Teague was doing what he was doing in the first place. You think there aren't a million and one parents out there just like my mother that would sell their children to a heartless industry. If anything, there are too many parents in this world like my mom, who are willing to sacrifice a child for profit or someone else's perversities. Like a … like a human sacrifice, forced to walk through fire and burn up as an offering to appease the false gods[18] of fame, hoping, just hoping that the gods will give them just another fifteen minutes of notoriety or another royalty check so they can afford to see another day and sacrifice all over again." Scott replies in anger.

"What are you even talking about? What is this human sacrifices and burnt offerings stuff? That is just a bit extreme don't you think? You act as if we're putting our daughters up for sale or something. Like you said, it was just a kid's show." AJ reaches for Scott but Scott pushes him away and walks out of the bathroom.

"Don't touch me! These are things you wouldn't understand because you see what you want to see. You manipulate what you believe in the same way you manipulate what your audience sees. It's why you think all of this," Scott lifts his hands and motions to the large bedroom, "is worth

---

[18] JEREMIAH 19:5 (NKJV)

saving. You've never known the value of human life." Scott replies as he walks to the bedroom door.

"Wait a minute! Stop treating me as if I'm the enemy here. I care about my children and I care about you. So why are we even arguing about all this?" AJ asks frantically.

"Do you care about our daughters enough to let all this go?" Scott asks, referring to the manor, the estate and the show but AJ does not respond. "I didn't think so." Scott replies before leaving the bedroom.

CHAPTER SEVENTEEN

After his argument with AJ, Scott makes his way to the guest room on the first floor. He pauses in the hallway when he can see a shadow cast of someone in the sitting room, beside the lit fireplace. It is late and the girls having gone to bed already, he figures it to be Margo that is still up. Scott enters the sitting room and finds Tristan in the chair nearest the fireplace, smoking a cigarette and staring intently into the flames. Tristan looks up and smiles and Scott realizes Tristan heard his argument with AJ.

"Everyone seems to be having trouble in paradise tonight." Tristan says as he flicks his ash into the fire.

"Maybe it's not really paradise like we thought?" Scott replies, as he remains standing while wanting to be alone but he does not want to leave Tristan unsupervised in the manor either. Scott did not know Tristan had come over tonight, and now he was wondering where Margo was.

"Well whatever it was, it was good while it lasted and I came into this relationship knowing it wasn't going to last very long." Tristan replies. "But I got a nice little gift out of it so it wasn't a total loss. What about you, marriage on the rocks or is this just a little hiccup?" Tristan asks smugly and Scott frowns.

"That's none of your business, and if Margo dumped you, why are you still here?" Scott asks. There was something about Tristan that Scott disliked from the moment he met him. Privately Scott was glad that Margo finally ended it.

"It's my last night here; I just wanted to take it all in before saying goodbye. I always wanted to light this fireplace, sit here, and relax with a drink and feel distinguished for once. I should have moved in here when she asked me to, before you all showed up, but I said no. I guess I didn't want to feel, what's the word? Domesticated; now that the option is gone I'm regretting not taking it and I'm too young to have regrets. You know I didn't mean to overhear, but I caught a little of what you said about human sacrifices." Tristan adds and Scott looks angry but Tristan raises his hands apologetically. "I said I didn't mean to overhear. It was just interesting to me what you said about the things some people will do to get what they want. It reminded me of something Margo said recently which also got me thinking; some sacrifices seem small at first in comparison to what you're after. I remember watching a movie when I was a kid about the Trojan War and that Helen woman that was supposed to be so beautiful. There was a scene where this king who was obsessed with Helen, wanted to launch his ships to get Helen back after she was kidnapped, or ran off, I don't remember which. I mainly remember this one scene about the ships, and how the king wanted Helen back so bad that he was willing to do anything and he and Helen weren't even a couple. So some guy shows up and he tells the king that if he sacrifices his own daughter, they'll get wind to launch their ships." Tristan chuckles to himself. "Isn't that something? The king actually killed his own daughter even though she was young, practically a baby, just for wind; and it didn't seem like it bothered him at all. It was absolutely worth it to him, to shed the blood of his little girl who trusted him, who believed that daddy would always keep her safe and instead he was the one who took her life, to fulfill his fantasies with Helen. They got the wind too, of course it was only for wind, not a victory in the war that came after, but the wind was enough." Tristan explains as he exhales cigarette smoke.

"Did they win the war?" Scott asks as he thinks about his own children, his daughters and his son. Tristan nods slowly while staring into the fire.

"I'm pretty sure they won. It was so long ago though, I don't remember the whole end but I do remember the king being killed at some point, so his dreams of claiming Helen as his own were short lived. I wonder if while he was dying he still thought it was all worth it. Oh well." Tristan replies as he tosses the remains of his cigarette into the fire and stands up. "I used to watch those gone too soon documentaries and one episode mentioned your old co-star Grayson, the islander boy. How his body was found in that motel room and the phone was off the hook in his lap as if he was trying to call for help. Maybe he was calling someone to talk him out of it, to tell him what all he had to live for. Who do you think he would've called?" Tristan asks with a knowing tone and Scott stares back at Tristan while recalling Grayson's silence on the other end of the line and then that strange pop.

"I'm sure we'll never know." Scott replies, refusing to give Tristan any information about Grayson and what fear drove him to do. As if knowing Scott is holding back, Tristan nods but says nothing more on the subject as he straightens his jacket and heads for the front door.

"It was interesting getting to know you and your family Scott, and I hope to see that pretty daughter of yours on the big screen someday." Tristan replies with a smile as he exits the house. Scott watches him from the window as he descends the steps and jumps into the car parked in the driveway.

"Is he gone?" Scott jumps and turns to see Margo standing behind him in her robe. Margo does not wait for Scott to answer but glances out the window herself to watch Tristan drive away.

"I really didn't want to give him that car, but it's not like I don't have another one and I felt so bad about everything, it was the least I could do. I mean I know we were using each other but I'm not completely heartless." Margo explains.

"I'm sure you gave him more than he gave you back Margo, so there's no reason you should feel guilty." Scott replies as he motions for Margo to sit in the seat Tristan left. Scott sits in the chair beside her.

"I think I feel more guilt about what I used to do with him. He got angry with me tonight because I wouldn't sleep with him anymore, isn't that silly, as old as I am and suddenly I'm all prudish and he's feeling rejected? If anything, I think it hurt his pride because I wasn't falling for his advances anymore and maybe he was worried he was losing his charm. Honestly, it had nothing to do with him physically, certain things have just been getting to me lately and I knew I had to let him go." Margo explains as Scott can tell she is holding back on her emotions.

"I'm sorry Margo; I didn't realize how much you liked him." Scott replies with genuine concern and Margo chuckles.

"Oh no, it wasn't hard because I liked him, actually my attraction to him started waning pretty fast after we met, he was just cute and young and gave me the time of day, but relationships have to be more than that. At my age, it can't all be about physical things and he isn't the talking type, at least not pleasant conversation. Although we did have one interesting chat that helped me to make up my mind but I'm just sad about change in general. It's strange that after talking to your daughter, I'm just not the same anymore." Margo replies.

"What do you mean? What does Kieri have to do with you and Tristan?" Scott asks.

"It's not as direct as you think, I just meant that I don't even read the Bible but Kieri and I were talking in the garden one day and I was left questioning everything I thought was normal. Then when Tristan and I were talking the other night, I found out that he doesn't believe in God. It seemed strange to me at first that someone would be so open about his lack of faith and I felt a little sorry for Tristan, but then as we talked a little more I realized that while I might believe in God, I wasn't doing much to show it. It's a little embarrassing to realize that an atheist does more in what they don't believe in than a lukewarm Christian like me does to glorify God. However, didn't Jesus say to be either hot or cold but if someone is lukewarm, He will vomit him or her back up?[19] I spent too much of my life trying to walk some kind of middle ground to not offend anyone while fooling myself into believing that I was going to heaven and this revelation has me questioning what I really believe in and what I really follow." Margo explains.

"How exactly are you supposed to *show* that you believe in God? And what's so bad about not trying to offend anyone?" Scott asks and Margo shrugs.

"Well I should be showing my faith in my actions for one thing. I'm coming to understand more and more about sexual immorality and how it's a sin. My time with Tristan was immoral and sinful, but I ran from that. It did feel wrong at times but I justified it to make it feel right until I saw Tristan's heart and I realized that he wasn't worth it. If I believe in God, I should believe in heaven and hell and if I believe in heaven and hell, I should believe that there are actions that dictate whether I go to one place or the other. Now as far as offense goes, that's a little more

---

[19] REVELATION 3:15-16 (NKJV)

complicated. People I know do things that go against God's word, so if I act as if what they do is right when God's word says it is wrong, how much faith am I showing in the word of God." Margo explains.

"Well I hope you're not blaming Kieri for that revelation, it's not her fault Tristan is how he is." Scott replies defensively.

"I'm not blaming anyone for anything; I just meant that it was a lot easier for me to live my own way and pretend that God doesn't see what I do or care that what I do is sinful. Although easier doesn't always mean better and when I had a little time to think about it, it made me feel somewhat grateful for Kieri. Now that I see things a little more clearly, I'm learning that regret can be a bigger, meaner monster than what I've dealt with in any of my stupid horror movies. Speaking of my films, there is another outlet that I never bothered to show my faith." Margo adds.

"How were you supposed to do that? Someone else wrote those movies and if you turned something down on principle they could fire you." Scott tries to comfort her.

"Yes, but there were other roles out there, parts that wouldn't have left me with guilt; I helped to normalize terrible things. I've made movies where women were degraded and abused and tortured in ways that no normal person should find entertaining but viewers are so desensitized they'll bring the whole family to watch people get raped and butchered right in front of them and then wonder where murderers get the motivation from. Some of those things happen to people in real life and yet we watch it on screen laughing and cheering as if it's funny. My jump-scare is someone else's everyday reality. Now while I understand that stories sometimes need reality, less vulgarity and visuals of perversity can go a long way in making that story well told and with an honest purpose. I could have said no to certain things or fought to drop a scene, but instead I sold myself, I let others use my body and I collected my check and went home. Little did I know what demons were following me. I don't blame Kieri for shining some light on what I tried to hide, more like I appreciate her for it because this house has been too dark for too long." Margo explains. "Of course Tristan and I weren't the only ones arguing tonight were we?" Margo asks and Scott shrugs.

"AJ and I always argue you should be used to it by now." Scott replies.

"Something's different about it this time around though. Were you and my brother fighting about the show?" Margo asks and Scott nods without saying anything. "I should've bet him money you wouldn't do it, but he wouldn't have paid up anyway." Margo quips.

"To be fair he almost convinced me. I don't know why but I was going to do it, at least for a moment for him and for Kieri. For a minute I thought maybe it would help her to see things differently." Scott replies and Margo frowns at him.

"See things differently how? You mean about her being a Christian?" Margo asks.

"It's been an issue, it still is but I don't know, I guess I'm just tired." Scott suggests and Margo stares at him.

"Maybe she's not the one who needs to see things differently? What are you going to do now?" Margo asks and Scott stares at her, perplexed by the question.

"What do you mean?" Scott asks.

"You know exactly what I mean. What are you going to do, about AJ and the girls, your marriage, your family?" Margo asks and Scott shrugs nonchalantly while trying not to show the panic growing inside of him at the realization that something has to change.

"I'm not going to do anything. Except maybe go home with or without AJ for now. Just because Kieri and I are not doing the show now doesn't mean we're not still a family, he'll join us when he wants to." Scott replies as he buries his hands in his lap to hide his agitation.

"I was referring more to how you're feeling now. You are not the same and like me I think you can sense that your relationship with my brother is not the same either and something is going to implode within it if it's not diffused soon." Margo replies and Scott scowls.

"Margo it's not that serious, we just had an argument, we have them all the time and it's not that big of a deal." Scott replies casually but Margo is not buying it.

"What about Kieri? She told me about the Bible study class and how she felt about having two fathers and I have to say that for someone like me who thought she believed in God and had her own relationship with Him, whatever I thought I was doing is nothing compared to your daughter. I never imagined someone being so bold as to stand up to her parents about God's word. I never stood up to my father about anything." Margo confesses and Scott looks weary.

"I guess I can be proud of her for sticking to her principles, but it's the one thing I worry about too. She has to understand that there are people in this world who don't take it well when you tell them they're going to hell." Scott replies with an expression of genuine concern for the safety of his daughter.

"I won't lie, talking theology with Kieri out in the garden the other day, hurt my feelings just a little at first. I never really thought of myself as an immoral or sinful person and I never really considered that God would care about what I was doing and with whom. Like my relationship with Tristan, at the time it was no big deal to me. I tried to brush the guilt off and tell myself, this girl is fifteen and she doesn't know what she's talking about. Then when I thought about it, when I really considered why she would even talk to me about God at all, I saw where it was coming from in her, a place of compassion and maybe even a little bit of fear for my salvation, even though she had just met me. We could all stay quiet about faith and never tell anyone about God and we could just live content and not think about what would happen to people when they die but then again, that's not love or compassion, in fact, that's not even care for another human being. If I love someone, it should matter to me that they have joy in this life and the next, I mean real, God-given joy and not what the world tells us is joy. It should matter to me where they go when they die. Talking to Kieri was the first time I ever felt like someone genuinely cared about me since before my mother died. Even though everything Kieri said to me was so seemingly indirect, I felt like God wanted me to hear it. After that, I really couldn't be angry with her. I couldn't see things the same way, and what Tristan was offering as love just didn't do it for me anymore. You're starting to see it too, I can tell and maybe it was easier for me because I've barely known Tristan a month while you've known my brother almost all your life and been married to him for nearly half that time. It would be like cutting off a piece of yourself, like dividing your own body in half." Margo explains and Scott looks down at the floor, knowing that what she is saying is a little too much honesty for him right now.

"AJ and I were never really one, at least not the way Kieri described God bringing two together as one, but you're right, because this is going to hurt and I don't think I can bring myself to do what I keep feeling like I have to do. What does God expect from people, to let go of everything they have ever known and just change with the snap of their fingers. I can't do that; I don't know anyone who can do that! I don't know what I'm going to do with my family now, I don't know what to do to make things okay again, if they ever were to begin with? I couldn't really see the flaws until Kyrie died; or at least up until that point I was afraid to address them." Scott replies as he flexes his hands, while trying to hold back the pain inside.

"That's the first time I've ever heard you say his name, you are changing and you're getting bolder, braver. Can I make a suggestion?" Scott nods but says nothing. "Don't go back, whatever you do, don't go back to the way things were. Don't run back to being ignorant and living your life like there is no heaven or hell because you don't want to be alone or because you think there won't be any consequences. Do not settle for what other people say should make you happy, just because it seems safe or familiar or common; living like that will only make things worse. You have to go forward and you have to stand up for yourself and your children. You are not the quiet little boy everyone can ignore anymore. You can't be afraid to address what is happening and has happened right in front of you if that's the only way to put a stop to it. You're a father now, which means you might have to get loud and be the voice of defense for yourself and your daughters that your mother never was for you." Margo explains as she places a hand on Scott's shoulder.

"Margo, this is my marriage and my daughters we're talking about. Does God just expect me to give up everyone and walk away? I love my girls." Scott cries out in frustration.

"Maybe He's not expecting you to give them up. So the real question is, what is He expecting of you?" Margo asks.

CHAPTER EIGHTEEN

When AJ wakes up late the next morning, alone in the guest room, he does not notice that Scott's belongings are missing. It is not until AJ finishes his shower that he observes Scott's toiletries are gone from the bathroom sink. Unconcerned with the missing bathroom items, AJ dresses and notes that Scott's clothes are no longer in the drawers or the closet. Only AJ's empty luggage remains propped in the corner of the room. Confused, AJ steps out into the hall and immediately heads to the first floor where he can hear voices coming from the kitchen. While passing the sitting room, AJ notices the full sets of luggage belonging to his family, resting by the front door. AJ enters the kitchen to find Margo, Scott, Kieri and Riah eating breakfast at the kitchen island instead of in the dining room. Margo notices him first and forces a smile.

"Well it's about time you woke up. Sorry we had to start breakfast without you but the food was getting cold." Margo explains and Kieri has to turn around to look at AJ as her back is toward the door. Riah is sitting on Scott's lap eating scrambled eggs and only stops to point excitedly at her Papa AJ. Scott does not look up from his cup of coffee.

"What is this, why are all your bags packed?" AJ asks and Kieri looks down at her plate saying nothing. Scott exhales and passes Riah to Margo.

"I'm taking the girls back home today. Our flight leaves this afternoon." Scott replies. AJ looks stunned.

"Excuse me. What do you mean you're taking the girls home? They are home; this is their home. This is our home." AJ says.

"I never agreed to stay here AJ." Scott replies.

"Then leave, but you're not taking my daughters with you." AJ counters.

"Kieri wants to leave too and I see no reason why Riah shouldn't come with her." Scott explains and AJ looks at Kieri then back at Scott.

"Is this some kind of joke? This is a joke right?" AJ asks as Margo stands up with Riah in her arms and walks past AJ. "Give her to me!" AJ orders but Margo swings away from him smoothly with Riah unfazed in her arms and glares at her brother.

"I won't! You and Scott need to talk and Riah is going with her Auntie Margo into the other room to finish her breakfast in peace." Margo replies while trying to keep her voice calm so as not to upset Riah who is still eating eggs with her bare hands off the plate in Margo's other hand. Margo leaves the room and AJ approaches Scott.

"So you just made the decision without me, to leave and take our daughters with you? What about our conversation the other night and everything we talked about? I thought we were going to work as a team now; what happened to that?" AJ asks.

"I was hoping that we could discuss this under different circumstances, but I think Kieri is old enough to understand that I'm leaving you." Scott says and even Kieri looks surprised. "I can't do this with you anymore and I want a divorce." Scott explains to AJ who steps back and looks at Kieri.

"Well that came out of nowhere. You want to leave too Kieri? You want to leave with Scott or is he talking *for* you again?" AJ asks Kieri.

"I don't like it here Dad." Kieri begins but AJ cuts her off.

"You don't like it here in this *house* or you don't like it here in this house with your *family*? I don't even know why I'm asking; of course, you have a problem with the house *and* your family because you have an issue with everything! Is it even possible to make you happy Kieri?" AJ asks in a patronizing tone and Scott stands up.

"Don't put words in her mouth and stop shouting at her AJ!" Scott counters and AJ turns on him.

"Oh, of course you have something to say because she's *your* daughter; I'm just the glorified nanny. You know what, I am happy to give you the space and the separation from me that you want so badly because you never respected me, and you taught our daughter to do the same every time you would undermine my parenting. Because I'm the big, bad, terrible father and you're the hero, you're the nice dad; you're the one Kieri loves even though you're the one who sent her away! I brought her back and she still loves you more!" AJ is on the verge of tears as he addresses Kieri. "What exactly did I do to you Kieri to make myself completely unnecessary in your life? Did I oppress you somehow Kieri?" AJ shouts at Kieri and Scott steps between them and pushes AJ away as Kieri begins to sob.

"Get away from her!" Scott snaps. "This is between me and you!" Scott says to AJ who pushes him back.

"There is nothing between you and me anymore, you're the one who wants the divorce and you can have it, but before you leave she is going to tell me exactly what I did to be treated like garbage by my own daughter that I love with everything in me! The daughter I saved from a life in foster care and becoming another black stereotype of wasted potential!" AJ addresses Kieri. "I gave you the best of everything I could and taught you to believe that you could do anything you set your mind to. Since you were a baby, I have been trying to protect you from cultural statistics and assumptions. Now after all that, you would rather follow some far-right Christians who use the same God to justify their own prejudice and hate toward people who look just like you! I gave you everything! I have done nothing but shower you with the love your own birth mother wouldn't give you. All I ever asked of you was for that same love in return, but you would never accept me as your father, not really, I can't compete with Scott to be your number one. Kaila returned that love and now she's gone and I have nothing!" AJ shouts with tears in his own eyes. Scott is still between them and AJ pushes him away as he turns to leave the kitchen.

"Kyrie!" Kieri whispers. AJ stops in the kitchen doorway and he and Scott look at Kieri.

"What did you say?" AJ asks.

"I said Kyrie! That's my twin brother's name, Kyrie. I was just correcting you." Kieri replies and both AJ and Scott are caught off guard by the calm in Kieri's voice. "Were you teaching Kyrie that *he* could be anything, when you were putting dresses on him and telling him that he could be the prettiest little girl? Were you battling the racist agenda of the far-right when you exposed my brother and me to gay pride parades and drag queen performances in adult night clubs? Places that were not made for children, where we saw people doing things that no decent human being would do in public, much less in front of a child. Did you think you were saving black lives when you took us to those marches and pro-choice rallies, while showing the world you were about women's rights too? I guess you've never seen the stats on how many innocent babies those clinics kill each year or care how many of those babies are black; whatever their race, maybe their lives only matter to God. You used my brother so that people would celebrate you for raising "woke" children and that is not love. Maybe you should look at who you are following Dad, and how much good it did for my brother to follow you. Then again, you could be right and some conservatives and so-called Christians do hate me for my skin, I don't know and I don't care; what I do care about is that you're my father and you claim to love Kyrie and me but all you ever showed him was hate. You showed him how to hate himself, how to hate God by rejecting how he was made and when he killed himself, you erased him so that even Riah doesn't remember him now. That is not what a parent is supposed to do and I hate you for that. I don't want to hate you, I don't want to hate anyone because I know it's wrong and I don't like the person it is turning me into. You two are the only parents I've ever had, and it hurts because I don't feel safe around you anymore Papa AJ." Kieri explains with tears in her eyes but AJ is the one who looks heartbroken.

After loading their bags in the car, Scott returns to the house and enters the woods to find AJ. After Kieri told him the truth, AJ silently left the kitchen and disappeared through the garden. Scott knew exactly where he had gone and found AJ standing over the now fallen statue in the clearing.

"What happened?" Scott asks as AJ stands with his hands in his pockets staring at the large figure, which is now face down in the dirt.

"I don't know, I got out here and found it like this. Maybe an animal knocked it over." AJ suggests without turning around to look at Scott. Scott studies the base of the statue and can see that no average animal could have gotten that statue out of the ground.

"I doubt even a bear could've done that." Scott says.

"What do you want? Don't you have a flight to catch?" AJ asks, still without looking at Scott directly.

"Yeah, Margo is riding with us to the airport to see us off." Scott replies.

"That's nice of her. I'm guessing she's selling the manor too, isn't she?" AJ asks and Scott nods before remembering that AJ is not looking at him.

"She didn't say specifically, but she might. I think it bothers her how your father got this house and what he did to keep it, what he did to expand it." Scott explains as Margo had confessed to him that she believed that her father was afraid the spirits of the children he exploited through the show were among the many ghosts haunting this house.

"She doesn't have any right to do that. This is my father's house." AJ replies.

"Your father is dead AJ and this is Margo's house, she can do with it whatever she wants." Scott reminds him.

"It's her house, but it should've been my house! I care more about this place than she does and Dad knew that and he was going to leave it to me instead. She took advantage of him being sick and she stole this house from me; she stole this land from me and now she's going to sell it when she has no right to, at least not morally." AJ replies and Scott turns to leave. "Is there someone else?" AJ asks and Scott pauses.

"What?" Scott asks.

"Is there someone else?" AJ repeats. "Are you leaving me to be with someone else, is that what this is all about? Because I know I haven't been … I know I wasn't always faithful to you and I made a lot of mistakes and I'm sorry but we don't have to do this. I swear I can do better, just give me a chance." AJ pleads as he finally faces Scott.

"There is someone else and it's over between us. I don't know Him that well but I'm trying to and He's helping me see that what we had, you and I, was wrong in so many ways and I have to go. This isn't forever, at least not in the sense of our family splitting up. You and I are over as a couple, our marriage is over, but I want Riah to know you and I want Kieri to forgive you." Scott explains and AJ scoffs but says nothing. "There is something else though. That statue, what it represents; I know what Axel is to you and how you see them, how you see *it*, because I saw Miranda the same way. She was the mother I always wanted and the father I never knew. I wanted to believe that she could help me and save me and bless me but she couldn't; she couldn't do any of those things because she was just a puppet, just like Axel." Scott points at the statue face down on the ground. "Axel can't do anything for you because Axel can't do anything for itself." Scott explains.

"You sound like Kieri. Are you going to tell me that her God can do for me all the things I look to Axel for? I don't need her God and I don't need yours and you don't know Axel like I do." AJ replies spitefully. Scott points at the fallen statue again.

"If that is the god you want, you might want to tell it to pick itself up." Scott replies before leaving the woods, AJ and his dead life behind.

EPILOGUE:

… THE LORD HAS TURNED IT FOR GOOD

"For what I am doing, I do not understand. For what I will to do, that I do not practice; but what I hate, that I do. If, then, I do what I will not to do, I agree with the law that it is good; but now, it is no longer I who do it, but sin that dwells in me. For I know that in me, that is, in my flesh, nothing good dwells; for to will is present with me, but how to perform what is good I do not find. For the good that I will to do, I do not do; but the evil I will not to do, that I practice. Now if I do what I will to do, it is no longer I who do it, but sin that dwells in me."[20] AJ reads the scripture in the obituary aloud with an expression of confusion. "I don't get it, what does that mean?" AJ asks as Scott removes their empty lunch plates from the table and sets them in the sink. Scott rests his hands on the edge of the counter and stares out the window at the long dead garden leading into the woods behind the manor for a few seconds before he turns around to face AJ.

"Well, for me, it meant that how I was living with you wasn't wrong to me until the word of God showed me the truth. After that, I hated the sinful things I was doing and wanted to do and thought about doing, mainly because those things were keeping me from God, and it was hard to focus on Him and do what He wanted me to do. I wanted to do His will but my flesh didn't and it had too much control. Does that make sense?" Scott asks and AJ frowns.

---

[20] ROMANS 7:15-20 (NKJV)

"Not really, but I can take it as nice poetry for now. So this was Margo's favorite scripture?" AJ asks as he turns the obituary over in his hands and studies the collage of photos taken over the last ten years of Margo's life after she left Stoddard Manor, noting that many of the photos featured his daughters as they grew up. Margo got to see more of Kieri and Riah then AJ did but even he had to admit that was his own decision and he had no one else to blame, except maybe Scott.

"It was; she was a fan of Paul's letters. She liked how he was a bad guy that became good. She called his story the best villain to hero arc she'd ever read." Scott replies as he tries his best to hold back the tears. He did not do very well at the funeral, even though he knew his sister-in-law had gone home, it meant that he would not see his friend anymore until his own time came. "Before she died, I asked Margo if she was scared. She said that like the apostle Paul, she was blind before and now she could see. She'd run the race, not as strong as him but she did it and she said she was ready to go home." Scott explains, as he recounts the final year of Margo's life as she balanced her chemotherapy treatments, medications and various appointments while living with Scott and his family, her family. AJ remains silent at first and Scott can see AJ's hand trembling slightly as his teardrops land on the laminated obituary. AJ quickly wipes his face and Scott turns back to the window overlooking the garden, pretending he does not notice.

"I'm sorry I couldn't make it to the funeral, I've just been really busy trying to keep this house together; and I've been having some trouble adjusting to my new medications this past week." AJ explains as Scott begins running the tap to fill the sink and has to wait a moment for the water to clear up. A few pipes burst last year and there was a lot of damage; even now, there was still a large water stain on the ceiling over the sitting room that was giving off a terrible smell. Scott offered to pay for the repairs but AJ was too proud to take his money and claimed each month that he would get it taken care of. For the last ten years, AJ had remained in this house alone. Margo moved out not long after Scott left and started over before she got sick. She allowed AJ to remain in the manor house rent free instead of selling it, but he had to manage the place on his own by paying the utilities and handling the maintenance while Margo handled everything else. When Margo got sick, AJ offered to take care of her at the manor but she declined knowing that her own brother's health was failing too and not wanting to be a burden to him. Margo did not tell AJ that she had no intention of moving back into Stoddard Manor under any circumstances. When Scott offered a spare room in his house, Margo quickly agreed.

After finishing the dishes, Scott clears the table of the food containers and leftovers and begins to shuffle the playing cards. This was their routine on the weekends when Scott managed to fly out for a visit every other month since AJ was diagnosed with HIV. By the time AJ began treatment he learned his immune system was badly damaged and he had reached the stage of acquired immunodeficiency syndrome. This was almost a year after Margo got sick herself.

Scott began visiting AJ to bring groceries when AJ's last live-in boyfriend disappeared after AJ's condition became visibly apparent. The weekend visits and the groceries were the most AJ would allow Scott to do, as he felt at times that he was inconveniencing Scott with the bi-monthly trips. Even after their divorce, AJ refused alimony or financial help from Scott, but would instead send money for the girls whenever he could. AJ continued to support himself with his online channel, rebranding himself and documenting his life with AIDs, or AHR as he called it, acceptance, healing and recovery.

"So is this supposed to mean that your life with me was what you didn't want to do but your body made you do it?" AJ asks sourly and Scott shrugs.

"It's a little more complicated than that but if that helps you understand the scripture, go with it." Scott replies as he begins to deal out the cards. On his trips out to see AJ, Scott would drop off the groceries and the two of them would have lunch together, and talk about their daughters over a game of cards. Before going back to his hotel for the evening Scott would ask AJ if he could pray over him and each time AJ would decline, Scott complied but he was not giving up. AJ had not seen his daughters on a regular basis since Scott took them away from Stoddard Manor. After their departure the girls only got to visit AJ once or twice a year for some holidays until AJ got sick and ended the visits altogether; admitting that he didn't want his daughters seeing him now or remembering him this way when he was gone. Scott himself was shocked at the sight of his ex-husband looking gaunt and emaciated. By now, AJ was at least forty or fifty pounds underweight and often tried to hide it by wearing large clothes and sweaters which just exaggerated his smaller frame.

"So your flesh wanted men but your faith didn't and your faith wanted ... women but your flesh wouldn't let you?" AJ asks sarcastically but Scott does not take the bait as he begins to sort his hand.

"Almost, but not quite." Scott replies.

"So how is the straight life working out for you? Are you still with Melody?" AJ asks and Scott can hear the bitterness in his tone. Scott had remarried four years ago and AJ was still upset about it and did not bother to hide it. When he and Scott separated, AJ had someone new a month later that he could not wait to show off to Scott in the background of his video calls with the girls and Scott never said a word; but as soon as Scott met Melody, AJ made a point of making Scott feel like he had done something wrong. Scott holds his hand up proudly showing off his gold wedding band.

"Still married and the straight life is treating me just fine." Scott replies as he tosses a card out on the table knowing by now how to play AJ's games.

"Well that's good. Are your church friends still fooled?" AJ asks as he plays his hand and Scott lays down his cards to show he won. AJ collects the cards this time and begins to shuffle.

"Fooled by what?" Scott asks as he has been waiting a long time for AJ to address the underlying issues. AJ glares at Scott as he shuffles.

"A person doesn't just change how they feel overnight. Anyone who would believe that you are suddenly straight because you found out that God doesn't like men together is an idiot and I'm not an idiot." AJ replies as he begins to deal.

"No, you're not an idiot, but neither are my friends or my wife. I'm not pretending to be in love with her, I am very much in love with her and I know you don't believe that but it's true. I didn't just turn straight overnight either. Leaving you was one of the most difficult things I've ever done, but I knew something had to change and I wasn't going to be able to change while still being attached to you. It wasn't so simple or quick and not everyone was very encouraging when they learned of the lifestyle I was coming out of." Scott explains as he recalls to himself the first men's Bible study he ever joined. They mocked and criticized him when he confessed to coming out of a gay relationship. AJ looks at him incredulously. "Eventually God led us to the church where He wanted us, the girls and I. I like the people there and I like learning about God. I appreciated that they were welcoming without letting me think that my old lifestyle was justified or that God was accepting of it, just so they wouldn't offend me. The more I learned about what Christ Jesus did to save me, the more intentional I became to stay on the right path. I was ready to be alone the rest of my life, just be a single dad to our daughters and never have any kind of relationship with anyone else if that's what it took for me to focus on God, leave my sins in the grave and raise our daughters the right way. In fact, marriage was the last thing on my mind, but God had other plans." Scott explains as he stares at his wedding band, recalling fondly the day he met Melody in a discipleship class he did not want to take in the first place. The core memory brings a glow to Scott's face and AJ has to look away when he can see the genuine joy.

"Well good for you while it lasts." AJ replies as he lays down his hand, which cannot beat Scott's cards.

"We're having a baby, I mean, Melody is pregnant. You're the first person I've told outside of Kieri and Riah. The baby is due in September." Scott adds cautiously. "I thought I should tell you now because I won't be able to visit as often to check in on you. Actually it may be a while before I can come back but Kieri and Riah would like to come down if you'll let them?" Scott says and AJ shakes his head.

"No, I don't need anyone to check on me, I'll be fine. I don't want to put them out, Kieri is working and Riah's got school and her sports, they have their own lives to live." AJ says, not wanting to remember the day when his family left and Kieri told him how she really felt. They still talked to each other afterward and the girls visited him as much as they could but AJ could not let Kieri's words go. Scott stops shuffling the cards as AJ goes silent.

"They want to see you. They want to make sure you're okay." Scott says and AJ shakes his head again.

"Well I'm not okay and I don't want them to see me like this. I don't want the girls to see me, not after everything that's happened and I don't want Kieri to interrupt her career for me. I will not do to her or Riah what my father did to Margo. Anyway, I guess congratulations are in order. Sorry I don't have any champagne or cigars to celebrate with." AJ adds, quickly changing the subject. "You're a little old to be a father again though aren't you? I mean Kieri's an adult now and Riah is going to high school soon; shouldn't you be done raising children. Or are you just trying to get it right this time around?" AJ asks while holding back tears.

"You know that's not what I'm doing AJ. We were surprised too. Melody thought she couldn't have children, she miscarried more than once when she was younger." Scott explains.

"Is she divorced too? I thought God didn't like when people got divorced, so why is He blessing you two?" AJ asks bitterly and Scott prepares a comeback but stops when he realizes AJ has been reading the Bible at some point, most likely, the one belonging to Margo's mother that Kieri found and Scott left behind on purpose.

"It is wrong under certain circumstances. Melody's not divorced though; by her own testimony, she was just reckless in her youth; and according to God's word, you and I were never really married, so I think she and I are okay." Scott replies and AJ looks away as Scott begins to deal. AJ refuses to pick his cards up but continues to stare at the wall.

"You say you love her, you told me you loved me too once." AJ says.

"I did love you, I do love you." AJ looks at Scott sharply. "I love you like a brother. I love you enough to come up here and make sure that you are still alive. I love you enough that I pray for you every day even when I remember our son every day and I want to hate you. I love you enough that I want our daughters to see you and forgive you. That is how much I love you but I'm starting to think it's not enough. Because my love doesn't seem to be helping you see how much God loves you and how patient He is with you." Scott replies and AJ quickly wipes the tears from his eyes and glares at Scott.

"If He loves me so much why is He trying to kill me? Why am I sick and rotting in this house alone? He loves me about as much as He loved Grayson." AJ says and Scott sets his cards face down on the table.

"God didn't make you sick, whoever you were seeing after we split up is the reason you're in this situation now so don't blame God for that, and you're alone because you choose to be. You know you have a lot of nerve bringing up Grayson, you know absolutely nothing about what happened to him or why, but I'm going to tell you what happened. Grayson got sick, he got scared, he got a gun, and he didn't give himself a chance. He didn't give God a chance. God gave me a chance because the same person that got Grayson sick was abusing me and I suspect abusing you." Scott replies and AJ inhales sharply but says nothing. "I wasn't there for Grayson, but I couldn't have helped him even if I was because I was too busy being bitter and angry like you are now. I was bitter that I was out of work, blacklisted, and hurt by the two people who knew that I was telling the truth but said nothing. One of them stayed quiet out of fear at first, but started to believe that his abuser could help his career, until his abuser infected him with a death sentence. The other had hopes of replacing me on the show and since his father would not give him what he wanted he fell under the manipulation of a pedophile that promised him his dream. And when that dream went to someone else, he got angry and decided to get back at everyone; from Teague to his father and anyone else who wouldn't make him the center of attention, by helping his grandfather set fire to a soundstage." Scott explains and AJ looks nervous. They both remain quiet for a moment before AJ speaks.

"How did you know?" AJ whispers.

"About the fire or Teague?" Scott asks but AJ remains silent. "I guessed Teague was abusing you because Grayson and I weren't the only children on the set that he was alone with. I wasn't sure because I couldn't understand, if you were being abused, why you would never tell your father but over time it all became clear."

"Allan never did anything that I said no to." AJ replies while not looking at Scott directly.

"You were a child AJ, even younger than I was and you didn't know how to say no; and he groomed you. He took advantage of you repeatedly and convinced you to sing his praises, and what's worse is that you weren't the only one that treated him like a hero. When Teague announced to the world that he was HIV positive, they celebrated him. No one asked about how long he'd known before going public for attention or who he'd been with before he said anything, who else he could've knowingly transmitted it to in that time? Everyone just acted like his diagnosis made him some kind of courageous pioneer and he was suddenly a national treasure to be praised. What exactly did he do to help the world in any way that was cause for celebration? There was nothing brave or noble about what Teague did to us." Scott replies as he recalls Grayson's fear all those years ago after they were tested together, while

Scott himself was only concerned with his own negative results at the time.

"My grandfather asked me to help him set the fire and I was so mad at my father. Allan told me that when I auditioned he suggested me as your replacement but Dad said no. I never thought you would be blamed for it. I didn't mean for that to happen. Please don't hate me." AJ pleads.

"I don't hate you AJ, not anymore, I mean I was bitter before, but now I'm grateful that God used what happened to end that part of my life for a very good reason. My point is that even after all the wrong we've done, God is not trying to hurt us, that's the devil's job. God is trying to talk to us and I believe everyone has a chance to hear Him and respond. I believe everyone has the chance to get the help they need from God, Grayson included, but he didn't know; he didn't know God and he didn't know he had a chance to live and heal because maybe no one told him. Maybe no one was praying for him the way Kieri prayed for us. I come out here because I'm trying to help you the way I couldn't help Grayson and the way I should've helped my son." Scott explains thinking about his anger at himself over the years and how desperately he just wanted to forget about AJ but God would not let him.

"Do you think I deserve forgiveness?" AJ asks.

"No AJ I don't; but neither do I. No human being deserves forgiveness, we don't even deserve life, but God gives them both and we need to take them as the gifts they are." Scott replies.

"After we divorced, Kieri asked me if it was her fault, and I did blame her at first for our separation. I didn't say it out loud when she asked me because I realized, I'm always blaming other people for my mistakes. I wasn't even faithful to you but I blamed her for our divorce, how pathetic is that. I know it was my fault, but what really made you leave me? What made you choose God?" AJ asks and Scott sits back in his chair.

"After Kyrie died and you left, I used to wander around the condo like a zombie because I couldn't sleep and one night I stopped outside of Kieri's bedroom and I could hear her reading a story to Riah. I sat on the floor in the hallway and just listened; she didn't even know I was out there. That night she was reading about this man named Gideon in the book of Judges and how God told him to pull down an altar that was on his father's property because the altar was for an idol,[21] a false god that was probably worshiped by the foreigners who were invading their land and stealing all their crops." Scott continues his explanation.

"Gideon didn't want to do it at first because he didn't want to get in trouble so he did it at night but the people found out anyway and they were going to punish Gideon but his father Joash showed up and intervened and he defended Gideon. I thought it was strange at first because the altar Gideon had torn down was on Joash's property and Joash wasn't even mad at Gideon for tearing it down. I didn't understand why Joash had it up in the first place if he was only supposed to be worshiping God. When I read that story again after I took Kieri's Bible, it occurred to me that maybe Gideon's father had the altar because he thought if the invaders saw it, they wouldn't take from his land or hurt his family. Maybe they would see that he worshiped the same false gods as them and leave him and his family alone." Scott pauses as he considers his own poor choices to blend in with the rest of the world, before continuing with the story.

---

[21] JUDGES 6 (NKJV)

"When Gideon pulled the altar down, I think Joash was reminded that he didn't need to worship fake gods because he had the one true God on his side. I think he was proud of Gideon and I was proud of Kieri for standing up to you, something that I could never do when it mattered most, when our son's life was at stake. I bowed to the world and I bowed to you for a long time because I thought I was doing the right thing by not speaking up. I actually thought I was protecting my family, but my fear kept me in bondage to the idea that I would lose everything all over again, or what I thought was everything. Conforming to the world cost me what was truly more important, our children, my salvation and knowing God now in life. Joash had to realize that if those false gods couldn't even defend themselves from Gideon pulling the altar down, how were they going to defend Gideon's family? I needed to realize that Miranda and what she encouraged could not help me with anything in real life. It was a painful lesson, but I wouldn't go back to what we had for anything in the world." Scott says.

"You should at least call the girls. I think they'd love to hear from you." Scott adds one last time as AJ walks him to his car. AJ smiles wearily.

"Maybe, I'll think about it. Will you give something to the girls for me? I found them in the attic among some of Margo's things." AJ explains as he hands Scott a small plastic bag with photos inside. The first few photos are of the twins before Kyrie transitioned. Scott handles the photos gently, recalling when AJ threw out all of Kyrie's old pictures to avoid offending Kaila. Riah could not remember what her brother looked like and even Kieri said she struggled sometimes to remember his face and the sound of his voice. "I must have sent them to Margo when the twins were young and just forgot all about it." AJ adds. Scott looks through the photos, takes the top picture of Kyrie out of the bag and hands the rest back to AJ.

"Call Kieri and Riah and then you can give them the rest of the pictures yourself." Scott replies. "They don't hate you AJ. They're not like us, bitter and broken, they understand what happened and they hold all their hate for the devil so they can have compassion on us." Scott replies and AJ nods but remains silent at first, not wanting his voice to crack and show how much he hurts inside and how scared he is.

"You know I think I like that Bible verse Margo liked so much. Maybe I can put it on my obituary too. I'm sure my funeral won't be too far off." AJ tries to joke to cover his own fear that he is not going to last much longer.

"The Bible isn't meant to be closing remarks to a life wasted. I know you've been reading it, so apply it now while you're still alive and breathing." Scott tells AJ as he hugs him tight, yet cautiously as AJ's small frame in his arms seems so fragile. AJ begins to cry onto Scott's shoulder but stops himself and pulls away quickly, turning away to face the house so Scott will not see the tears in his eyes.

"You drive safely and call me when your plane lands. And … and good luck to you and Melody and the new baby." AJ replies with his back to Scott as he hurries back into the manor before he breaks down completely.

AJ watches Scott in front of the house for a moment as he climbs into his rental car and pulls out of the driveway. When Scott's car is out of sight, AJ walks through the kitchen, enters the garden and makes his way carefully along the cobblestone path, knowing that in his condition, this is not a good idea but he has to go. Last night AJ had a dream that he was on a beach, Oliver's beach and AJ stood on the coast with his feet in the sand as the tide rolled in up to his ankles, just waiting, waiting for something or someone. Off in the distance he saw something in the ocean, as it drew near AJ was overcome with this sense of dread and when the body washed up, AJ understood why. It was a strange looking figure, like a doll but larger, a puppet. It took him a moment to realize that this was Axel the Merperson, or the puppet version except the body looked as if it was decomposing. AJ woke in a cold sweat and could not get back to sleep that night. When Scott arrived the next morning, AJ desperately wanted to tell him about the dream but he held back.

When AJ enters the clearing, the destruction does not surprise him, but it does frighten him, like the dream he somehow expected this. The statue was destroyed; shattered into countless pieces of precious metals not much larger than gravel and scattered all over the clearing. AJ could see that some chunks of the statue still held their gold plating but the rest looked like scorched pieces of various metals. He did not know what kind of tool could do this. The tarp lay in a pile, cast off to the side and AJ would not dare to touch any of it. He just stood there staring at the destruction and eventually began to sob.

AJ did not know how long he had been in the woods but when he returned to the house, the sun was beginning to set. AJ sits at the kitchen island and pulls his cellphone out of one pocket and the old photos out of the other. Setting both on the island, without thinking, AJ dials Kieri's number, a part of himself hoping she will not pick up. She answers immediately and AJ almost loses his nerve when he hears her voice.

"Hi Dad!" She says cheerfully. AJ's voice catches in his throat.

"Hi Kieri, how are you?" AJ asks.

"I'm great now. How are you?" Kieri asks with genuine excitement in her voice.

"Oh I'm still me," AJ replies playfully. "It's so good to hear from you. Your father just left here and I just … I just wanted to hear your voice." AJ replies.

"Oh I wish Riah was here. She's actually out of town at a track meet or a basketball game, I can't remember which but I know she'll be back at Dad's house on Sunday. I can text you her number if you want it? You should see her, she's a natural athlete, she does basketball, water polo, and track and field and she's almost as tall as Dad, I mean almost as tall as Papa Scott." Kieri explains.

"That's amazing; maybe I'll give her a call tomorrow. So I hear you auditioned for a show." AJ says and he can hear Kieri sighing on the other end.

"Well I did and I got the part but I had to turn it down. At first everything seemed pretty straight forward but when it came time for the contract, well, they wanted to make some changes at the last minute." Kieri explains.

"What kind of changes?" AJ asks.

"Well, it's a little embarrassing but, they offered me more money to do some nude scenes, mostly topless they said, as if that makes it better and they said something about modest sex scenes, whatever that is. Anyway I told them no and I think my agent is mad at me; this is my third agency in two years. And I know what you're going to say: That I should take the money and just do it and stop letting silly morals get in the way." Kieri adds playfully. AJ listens with disappointment as he realizes those are his words; and how much he sounds like his own father. AJ rests his hand on the photo of Kyrie and Kieri in their uniforms for their first day of school.

"I'm proud of you." AJ replies and Kieri goes silent on the other end. AJ can tell she is still listening though. "I'm really proud of you for sticking to your principles and knowing your worth. Taking a role like that is not something you would want your family to see you doing and it's not something you could be proud of. Don't lose that strength of yours Kieri or your morals; there will be other roles, better roles." AJ replies.

"Thanks Dad." Kieri says after a moment. "I love you." Kieri adds and AJ's eyes burn with tears.

"I love you too, and Riah and Kyrie. I need to say that I'm sorry for everything that has happened between us. I never meant to hurt any of you, I do love you all very much, and I always will. I don't believe that apologies change anything but I don't know how else to say that I was wrong and that I've done something terribly wrong. I wouldn't blame you if you said no, but I would love to see you both, you and Riah. Maybe next month when summer starts you two can come out for a visit, and you'll both be back before the new baby arrives." AJ adds as his heart is pounding in his chest. He can practically see Kieri smiling on the other end.

"I'll always love you Dad and that sounds like a great idea." Kieri says and AJ exhales, feeling a weight come off him suddenly.

"Well I'll let you go, but I'll give you a call later this week. Can I ask you a favor though, will you pray with me?" AJ asks and Kieri does not hesitate.

"Of course I will." Kieri replies. AJ is unsure of what to do but simply closes his eyes as his daughter speaks intercession for him just as she has been doing for years. After Kieri prays, AJ speaks his own words, asking God to forgive him as he remembers the last time he spoke to his son, just before Kyrie took his own life. Kyrie confessed to AJ that he was afraid and doubting things. He could not understand why his body was rejecting his transitioning. AJ now understood that Kyrie's body was trying to heal itself of the wounds AJ had made. As his past is brought to the surface piece by piece, that feeling that was once upon AJ that he could not be forgiven begins to melt away. If Kieri can have compassion on him now, how much greater is the compassion of God? AJ had seen the wrath of the God he did not believe in before, now he was feeling the mercy of the God he knew to be real.

~

"Therefore I exhort first of all that supplications, prayers, intercessions and giving of thanks be made for all men, for kings and all who are in authority, that we may lead a quiet and peaceable life in all godliness and reverence. For this is good and acceptable in the sight of God our Savior, who desires all men to be saved and to come to the knowledge and wisdom of the truth." – **1 Timothy 2:1-4**

ABOUT THE AUTHOR

Dawn Nicole Evans was born and raised in Southern California. She grew up a book nerd and spent an unusual amount of time in the library. While reading was one of her passions, a love for writing her own stories followed close behind.

It was not until her late twenties that Dawn found her way to church to hear the Word of God and it would change her life forever. Years later she would begin to dive into her calling of writing about the excellence of God and the good things in life that are sometimes harder to see.

Her focus is on encouraging others in different seasons of life to keep up hope and to know that God's Word is not invalid or outdated in any way, but may just be more crucial now to our lives than ever before.

ALSO BY DAWN NICOLE EVANS

~ 225 ~

TOMORROW CAN WORRY ABOUT ITSELF (2021)

SPOTS IN YOUR LOVE FEASTS (2022)